Coveting the Dream

Coveting the Dream

JACINTHA P. GRIFFITH

Katamja Press
McKinney, Texas

Coveting the Dream

© 2012 Jacintha P. Griffith

First printing 2012

ISBN 978-0-9856556-2-4

LCCN: 2012940906

ATTENTION CORPORATIONS, UNIVERSITIES, COLLEGES, AND PROFESSIONAL ORGANIZATIONS: Quantity discounts are available on bulk purchases of this book for educational and gift purposes, or as premiums for increasing magazine subscriptions or renewals. Special books or book excerpts can also be created to fit specific needs. For information, please contact Jacintha P. Griffith by email at: tucksee@att.net

Interior and cover design by Juanita Dix
cover images courtesy of istock.com ©2012

Chapter 1

Serena gasped as she stepped into the river. It was colder than she had imagined. She couldn't see her body below her waist; the water was as dark as the sky hanging above it. The reflection of the lights from the walking bridge above danced on the surface of the water in lines and circles, but did not penetrate the darkness beneath it. Her heart was beating faster now as she stared at the expanse of water ahead, pondering how deep it dropped. She did not know how to swim, and could easily be pulled downstream if the current was even mildly rapid in the middle. Miguel, tall and muscular, had entered the river first. "Don't worry, señora, there is a rope," he whispered, sensing her fear. Behind her, another man was helping a woman, older than she was and carrying a baby, to step from the river bank into the water.

Earlier, while they were hiding in the bushes in the darkness on the bank of the river, Serena had watched in disbelief as the woman wrapped a small cotton blanket around the infant boy who wasn't more than three months old. She then placed him into a small, black, plastic bag held open by one of the men, the opening of the bag clung around the baby's shoulder. Next, she gently packed the baby inside a back-pack. The same man tightened the straps on her back while she tucked two small blankets, one on either side of the baby, and finally she positioned his face upward near the opening

1

of the backpack. She then filled a dropper with green liquid from a small bottle she had removed from her pants pocket and squeezed it into the baby's mouth. She looked at Serena, smiled and said, "To make him sleep."

The woman also gasped when she entered the cold water that reached her waist. But the men were unfazed, silent, intensely preparing for the mission. They were now all in a line in the water; Miguel in front, one man behind him, then Serena, the woman with her baby and behind her the two men who were the last to join the group. Miguel whispered instructions in a low, flat voice. He spoke in Spanish, then repeated some things in broken English. He tried to assure them that the water was not much deeper in the middle. He beckoned them to hold onto the thick rope just beneath the surface of the water, and to move forward only when he directed. If the guards patrolling above shined lights into the water, they were to quickly submerge until the lights passed over them. Serena understood now why they were all required to wear dark clothing.

When Miguel stopped speaking, the woman behind Serena exclaimed in a nervous whisper, "Ay-dios-Mio, my baby," and made the sign of the cross touching her forehead, the backpack and her shoulders. Sensing her fear, Miguel moved to her place in the line, and showed her how to pull the opening of the plastic bag from around the baby's shoulders to over his head, gathering and twisting it. "Hold the twist so that no water gets into the bag," he said, then reassured her that there would be enough air for the tiny child to breathe, if they had to submerge under the water. Serena could not believe the risk the woman was taking with her baby, especially since it was well known that there had been some tragic situations in the past as others had tried to make this unlawful entry.

As they waited for Miguel to give the command to move on, she realized that her need to do this had become so desperate that even a possible tragic end to the journey would not have deterred her. She began to think about the time the desperation inside of her was ignited and became like a flame she couldn't put out. And the memory of Aunt Julia's words of caution about forcing her way into closed doors, sent shivers through her body as she stood in the cold, dark water.

🙚🙠

It was the rainy season in Belize. Rain had been falling non-stop for three days, pounding roofs with a fury. The wind rattled the shutters on the windows, relentlessly noisy day and night. Serena stared out the window at the dark, gloomy outside. She felt depressed, trapped too long indoors by the weather that could trigger dangerous mud slides, overflowing rivers and treacherous roads.

The house was silent as Serena turned and looked around the room. Her son was having his afternoon nap in her bedroom, Aunt Julia was in the kitchen grating coconut to make oil, and Uncle George was sitting in his favorite rocking chair in the living room smoking his pipe, his eyes closed. Tobacco helped calm him during these restless times indoors; he was a hard-working farmer, his once tall upright posture now hunched from years of bending to tend the soil. To him, it seemed longer than three days, waiting for the storm to pass, worrying about the effects of the rain storm on his land, the crops and livestock. Every year when the hurricane season began, or when there was mention of a hurricane, Uncle George would say, "Oh boy, I hope we don't get another Janet." Then he would proceed to go on and on about hurricane Janet in 1955, and how it had devastated parts of the country. Serena had experienced only one terrible hurricane; it was hurricane Greta a year ago. It had moved through the central Caribbean, turned into a category four hurricane when it neared the coast of Honduras, and made landfall at Stann Creek district causing major damage to the southern coast of Belize.

When Serena turned back to stare out the window and at the rain, she thought of her boyfriend Nick who had been gone now for 18 months. It had been six months since she last received a letter from him. She missed him, and was beginning to fear that he had abandoned her and their son Benjamin. She was also worried that something awful may have happened to him and she had no way of knowing. The letters came often in the first few months he was away, with money and promises that they would be together again as soon as he had a place for them and enough money for their airfare. But as time passed, the letters came less frequently, and there were fewer expressions of love and missing her and his son. Tears were beginning to fill her eyes when the sound of soft footsteps jolted her. She turned around. "Hi honey," she said, now smiling slightly. Benjamin smiled back and lifted his arms. She reached down, picked him up, squeezed him gently, and kissed him. He was 24 months old now and had the handsome features of his father.

That third night of the storm, Serena had a difficult time falling asleep thinking about Nick and the uncertainty of her future. Memories began replaying in her mind and she couldn't make them stop. Hours passed and soon the roosters' crooking signaled daybreak. She heard some commotion in the yard. Looking out her bedroom window, she saw that the sky was still overcast, but the rain was now only a drizzle. As soon as Uncle George opened coops, the chickens trampled on each other to get out to freely roam the yard. They ran madly around, clucking and pecking at the soggy soil that made the earth worms, easy prey. The yard looked as if a bulldozer had driven through and had pressed the flower plants into the wet ground, and most of the top soil had been washed away. There were puddles of water and tiny streams everywhere around the house as the water continued to flow down from the hill behind their home.

Her son was still asleep, so Serena put on her robe and went into the kitchen where her aunt was standing at the stove frying cod fish cakes for breakfast. She put her arms around her aunt's shoulders and kissed her on the cheek. Aunt Julia didn't care much for touching and hugging, Serena had never seen any outward show of affection between her aunt and uncle.

She sat on the stool next to her aunt for a few moments, and then finally got the courage to say, "I've been thinking about Nick a lot, I'm not hearing from him, and I'm worried."

Without looking up her aunt asked, "How long has it been since his last letter?"

"It's been about six months, and he's been gone now 18 months," she answered, solemnly.

"I would be worried too." Aunt Julia looked at her and sighed. "Promises are often broken, my dear."

There was a long silence between the two of them.

🦋 🦋

"Okay, let's go, the guards are at the other end," Miguel whispered excitedly.

Miguel's command brought Serena back into the moment. She didn't know how long they had been standing in the river, but her toes were beginning to burn from the frigid water and her skin was beginning to itch under her tight, wet jeans. The group began to make their way across, holding onto the thick rope that was just below the surface of the water and must have been attached to very strong objects on each bank. After she had moved a few feet, the water rose higher up on her body and the mud at the bottom of the river felt softer under the Timberland boots she was given to wear. As Serena looked at the dark, murky water, fear suddenly gripped her as she remembered the water snakes in the rivers in Belize. She took a few deep breaths to calm the panic rising up inside of her. They were about half of the way across, when Miguel halted and whispered to stop. He pointed up to the bridge above. "The guards are walking back to the other side now, we can't move until they pass over us."

Miguel had a keen sense of everything around him, so critical for his choice of work. The others did not hear the footsteps but they did as he commanded, waiting tense and motionless. No lights from above searched the water below. Then, with urgency in his voice, Miguel urged them to move faster to get to the opposite side before the guards started their routine pace back.

The water was halfway up Serena's chest now, and moving a little more rapidly. She could feel her body being pushed by the current as they trudged along, hearing only the ominous rippling of the water around them. Suddenly, the woman with the baby made a low, frightened groan. When Serena looked back, the woman had let go of the rope and was drifting away from the line. Miguel quickly began making his way towards her and whispered in a harsh tone, "What's the matter with you señora?"

"I felt something on my leg." She responded nervously.

The current was pulling her farther away from them. She was clutching onto the backpack with one hand, and the other was outstretched for help. Miguel grabbed hold of her hand and began pulling her back toward the line. He was tall, strong, and well-built, but needed help pulling her back against the current. The other men sprang forward and formed a chain, pulling Miguel and the woman back to the rope.

"Could be anything, señora, don't forget you are in a river," Miguel said, as everyone took their position in the line.

The woman began to cry softly so Miguel led her to a new position in line, directly behind him. When Miguel, who remained calm, resumed his leadership of the line, he looked up at the bridge, listened and said, "Please, let's move faster." The guards appeared to be lingering on the opposite side, but the urgency in Miguel's voice made them push their cold, weary legs through the water.

"Let's get out of the water before they come back," Miguel commanded when they were a few yards from the bank.

No longer needing the rope, they followed him along the shore line of the river where the water was shallow and calm. They went under the bridge and continued to walk in the shallow water, until Miguel stopped and pointed to the embankment. Climbing out of the water was difficult. The men lifted the woman with the baby up and onto the embankment, and then Serena was next. Both she and the woman were on their hands and knees crawling up the slope in the darkness, trying to find a good place to stand upright. Serena's legs were tired; they felt heavier because of her wet clothes and boots. The men pulled and pushed each other up out of the water, laughing quietly as they slipped and slid, struggling to get up the rocky embankment. Miguel, the last to get out of the water, led the way through the dense low bushes; he appeared to be sure of every step he took in the darkness. It was about midnight, the moon was directly above them providing only dim light through seams in the clouds covering it.

They walked for about 10 minutes along a rocky path of dried grass and shrubs, the outline of a high wall could be seen off in the distance. The path eventually changed and they were going down-hill, which was easier on Serena's tired legs. Miguel led them to an area of low trees and thick shrubs, where he stopped and removed some cut tree branches to reveal a dark opening in the ground. "I go first, and one at a time please," he said as he dropped himself into the opening and began to crawl into the dark hole. He waited until he was a few feet inside before turning on a small flashlight, which barely illuminated the darkness of the tunnel.

They followed, crawling on their hands and knees, slowly, try-ing to avoid bumping into each other. The ground was dry, hard, and painful on their hands and knees. The tunnel reeked of burnt cigarettes and urine. When they finally stopped, Miguel instructed them to sit and wait. In the darkness, the six strangers huddled to-gether, wet, cold and anxious as they realized that they were now at the most critical part of the journey. They heard the sound of traffic in the distance. Miguel used the small flash light to locate a large duffle bag. He opened it and gave them each a small woolen blanket to wrap around themselves to keep warm. Serena helped the woman sitting next to her to cover herself and the baby.

"We have to wait for the signal," was all that Miguel said as they sat in silence and waited. He was a man of few words, direct in his instructions and deliberate in his movements. No one dared to ques-tion him.

❧ ☙

Serena fixated on the dark tunnel walls, looking to see if any-thing moved. She was terrified of bats and anything that crawled.

She pulled her legs up and rested her chin on her knees. In the darkness, no one moved except for the woman. She lifted the baby out of the backpack and removed the plastic bag from around his body. She brought the face of the sleeping child next to hers, kissed him gently and whispered, "Mi Amore," before repositioning him in the backpack with only the blanket wrapped around him.

That tender moment between the woman and her baby prompted Serena to think about her son Benny, sleeping now, alone in the bed they used to share. She imagined him crying, she had never been away from him. Before leaving the house at six o'clock the previous morning, she had picked him up while he was asleep, hugged and kissed him several times before reluctantly putting him back in bed. Now, in the tunnel, the realization of what she was about to do scared her. If something tragic happened to her, Benny would lose his mother at an early, vulnerable age, just as she had lost her own mother.

The memories of her mother had faded over the years, but she couldn't forget the tragedy as it was told to her when she was old enough to ask. Serena often wondered what would be different about her life, if her mother had not been taken from her when she was only three. She had not heard from her father in many years. There was no memory of what he looked like; she had no pictures. He had been a British Soldier stationed at the border between Belize and Guatemala. When she learned that her father was British, she finally understood that it was because of that heritage she had the lighter skin tone, hazel colored eyes and black, wavy hair, in the otherwise predominantly Creole community of darker skin tones and tightly curled hair. Her childhood friend Valerie called her "Vanilla" because of her lighter complexion.

Serena's mother, who was only 24 at the time of the accident, worked as a nanny with a well-to-do family in Belize City, and came home to San Ignacio on the weekends. It was on a Friday evening when the accident occurred on the Hawkesworth suspension bridge. Serena's father had picked her mother up on his motorcycle from the bus stop. They were driving on the one lane bridge when they col-

lided with a car driven by a drunken motorist. Her father had suf-
fered several broken bones, but her mother who was not wearing a
helmet, sustained a severe head injury and died two days later at the
Karl Heusner Memorial Hospital in Belize City.

Soon after the accident, her father returned to England for intensive rehabilitation and never returned to work in Belize. For about
the next five years, Aunt Julia received letters and money from him
about twice a year, and always at Christmas. But the letters stopped
coming about 10 years ago. Although her aunt and uncle, who had
no children of their own, took very good care of her, Serena always
felt as though something was missing. She often watched longingly
as her friends were embraced by the big, strong arms of their fathers,
and kissed lovingly by their mothers. As she got older Serena longed
for the connection that had been severed with her mother. Then, at
last, Nick came along and filled the empty spaces in her heart with
kind words and loving caresses that made her feel like she belonged
to someone. Now, in spite of Aunt Julia's warnings about the dan-
ger of entrusting her life to strangers, ruthless men who would not
protect her if things went wrong, as she waited with the others for
Miguel's next command, she reasoned with herself that Nick was
worth the risk.

❧❧ ❧❧

Miguel's sudden movement brought Serena back to the moment. He crawled to the opening, moved some scrubs and looked
out, then turned back and whispered to the group, "He's here!" They
gathered around him at the opening and looked out. Beyond the
scrubs and low bushes about 200 yards away, there was a two lane
highway that was not well lit. The street lights were far apart from
each other. The opening of the tunnel was in an area of darkness
between the street lights. A white van was parked in the lit area closest to them, but not directly under the light pole. The driver stepped
out, unlocked the side door facing them and left it just a little ajar.
He walked to the back of the van and began removing a spare tire

from its holder underneath. Miguel began to give instructions. He decided the order in which they would leave the tunnel; the woman with the baby would leave first. He instructed them to run quickly, get into the van and remain low to the floor. If they saw the headlights of a vehicle approaching, they were to lay low in the grass and wait for it to go by before proceeding.

The woman with the baby darted quickly through the shrubs, climbing the incline to the street. Then she slipped and fell. Miguel put both hands on his head and swore quietly. The woman pushed herself up and made it into the van just as the reflection of headlights signaled the approach of a car in the northbound lane. Two of the guys left the tunnel shortly after the car drove by; Miguel reminded them to remain low in the van, covered under the blankets. Just as Serena was about to leave the tunnel, Miguel pulled her and she tumbled back into the tunnel. "Wait" he whispered urgently. When she sat up and looked in the direction of the van, a police car was pulling up behind it. Miguel put his hands on his head again and swore under his breath. The remaining three in the tunnel looked on anxiously as the policeman got out and approached the man changing the tire, one hand on his pistol and the other holding a flashlight.

The man stood up, he appeared to be calm as he gestured with his hands and pointed at the tire. The policeman looked around as the flashing lights of his patrol car was illuminating the isolated area. He began to walk toward the front of the van. "Ay-dios-Mio," Miguel whispered nervously. Just then a voice echoed on the radio in the patrol car. The policeman walked back to the car, reached in and began talking into the radio. He gestured with his hands and said something to the man who was now squatting and mounting the spare tire onto the wheel, then he quickly got into the car and sped away with the lights still blaring. Serena was shaking from the anxiety she felt at that moment. Miguel exhaled loudly, "That was close."

The three still in the tunnel waited until the man had bolted the tire onto the wheel, then they raced through the shrubs and into the van. They all remained still and covered. After a few minutes, they felt the rear of the van being lowered, and soon afterward the man opened the driver's door, turned the engine on, and yelled, "Welcome to America, seniors y senoras!" They tossed off the blankets, leaped from their crouched position, sat in the seats and cheered. Miguel climbed into the front passenger seat, he and the driver exchanged, "high fives," laughed out loud and began speaking to each other in Spanish. The rest of the group behind them was quiet, relieved, happy, but too tired for conversation.

Thirty minutes later, the van pulled into the dimly lit parking lot of a three-story brick apartment building. Serena was so tired that she had to be helped out of the van by Miguel, using his strong, muscular arms to lift her down. During the ride, she had dozed off; so did some of the others. Clutching the blankets tightly around them against the cold night air, they followed Miguel to a first floor apartment. Once inside, they were instructed to be as quiet as possible. The three men, relieved that they were safe, began speaking with each other for the first time in hushed tones as Miguel had commanded. The driver of the van had followed them into the apartment. He whispered briefly in Spanish to Miguel, who handed him an envelope, then he left the apartment closing the door quietly behind him.

They sat on the floor of the large open room, which was empty except for pillows and quilt comforters on the floor. Six duffle bags of varying sizes were stacked neatly in one corner; Serena recognized her bag, she had last seen it at Juanita's little cement house in Tijuana. The bags with their personal belongings had been delivered to the apartment before their arrival by another member of this well organized team of smugglers. As everyone claimed their bag, Miguel again instructed them with calm, confident leadership. He pointed first to the door of a bedroom where the women were to sleep, then to the tiny bathroom where the women were to shower first. After the men had showered they were to make themselves comfortable on the floor in the living room, using the pillows and blankets. He handed them each a towel and wash cloth from a linen closet near the bathroom door.

Once in the bedroom, Serena helped the woman unhook the straps of her backpack with the baby still asleep in it. When she took him out of the bag, his clothing was slightly damp and very warm. While the woman showered, Serena carefully wiped the baby's face with a warm, wet wash cloth. He stirred, made a sound and peeked out of his right eye for only a few seconds. She changed his diaper and dressed him in the clean clothes his mother had laid on the bed. As she swaddled him in a dry blanket and held him, he continued to sleep, breathing quietly. She stared at the face of innocence, smiled and whispered, "Little man, today you made an unlawful entry."

It was almost 2.30 a.m. when Miguel tapped lightly on the bedroom door. Teresita was sitting on one side of the bed breastfeeding her baby, and Serena was lying on the opposite side of the bed ready for sleep to take over her tired body. "Senoras, would you like something to eat?" Serena forced herself to get up and opened the door. Miguel, in clean clothes, his jet black hair wet and clinging to his head, held out a plate with two sandwiches and two small bottles of orange juice. She looked past him and the three other men were sitting on the floor eating and speaking softly to each other. "Thank you, I am so hungry!" Teresita announced from inside the bedroom. Serena accepted the offer, although more than anything she wanted to go to sleep. The women sat stoically, side by side on the bed, eating together in the dimly light room after the baby had been placed in the middle of the full size bed to sleep.

Teresita turned and looked at her sleeping baby and began to cry. Sensing Serena's concern, she whispered, "Tears of joy." In a tone barely audible, she told her story: She had made the journey to be with her husband, Juan, who had left Guatemala almost 12 months ago. It had taken him four days by bus and van from Guatemala to Tijuana, since they couldn't afford an airplane ticket, and he needed to save the money for living expenses until he found work. They had planned for her to join him soon after he got settled, but soon after he left she discovered that she was pregnant and decided not to risk her pregnancy by taking such as potentially treacherous journey.

She described in fairly good English her longing for Juan, the loneliness, and the hardship of the pregnancy without him. "I would go through fire to be with my Juan," she said with such passion that Serena felt a quiver in her stomach. "I was not going to leave my baby behind either." She was crying softly again as she talked about children in her small town who hadn't seen their parents in years, and were being raised by friends and relatives. They were left behind by parents who intended to be reunited with them shortly, but were unable to go back to get them. Serena felt a pang of guilt. She had left Benjamin behind, and the thought of not seeing him, indefinitely, scared her. She listened without comment, and when Teresita was quiet, she climbed into the side of the bed against the wall, being careful to give the baby and mother plenty of room.

❧ ☙

The sleep that she desperately wanted now evaded her. Serena lay awake in the corner of the bed, staring at a thin line of light reflecting into the room from the space between the window frame and the vinyl shade. In the silence of the apartment, she could hear the rhythmic breathing of Teresita, who was already asleep. She had never experienced this before, so tired and yet unable to fall asleep. She had been up since four a.m. the day before, racing from one stop to the next, anxious about following instructions and not missing connections. She had started out by getting on the first bus from San Ignacio to Belize City; it was a two-hour ride. With no direct flights between Belize and Mexico, she had to travel by buses, and spent most of the day with her emotions in high alert fearing she would miss one bus or another.

The man with whom she made initial contact, had told her that if she missed any of the connections to return to her home immediately. There was no room for mistakes, he had said, and no one would be waiting around for her. There was something sinister about him that scared her at that first encounter. He never looked directly at her as she sat across from him at the restaurant where they met. He wore a hat that covered his entire forehead and spoke only in short sentences. He had instructed her over the phone to bring a picture of herself and her passport to their first meeting at the restaurant. A week later she met with him for the second time. He returned her passport and she gave him the second half of the fee. His instructions were to travel with only a large backpack, and to wear black jeans and a black tee shirt on the day of travel. Without explaining, he asked for her shoe size. He then told her what to say at each stop and promised that his people would take care of the rest.

When she arrived in Belize City that morning, Serena made her first connection on time. She took the Northern Transport bus from the terminal, which traveled along the Old Northern Highway. The bus stopped at Corozal, picked up and dropped off passengers, then headed to Santa Elena's, the border crossing town on the Belizean side. She presented her passport to the Belize immigration there, stating calmly that she was going to Mexico to visit friends. The bus continued to Chetunal's terminal in Mexico. She again made it through the Mexican immigration, showing her passport with a stamped Mexican visa on the second page. Serena left the immigration line just in time to catch the bus leaving for Cancun Aeropuerto Internacional, where she got on an Aeromexico flight from Cancun to Mexico City. The plane landed 15 minutes later than scheduled, so she had to run through the terminal to the departure gate to board the American Airlines Flight from Mexico City to Tijuana International airport. She was the last person to walk into the airplane; it was as if they were waiting for her.

She had been instructed to wait near the exit doors of the terminal, but was not given a description of the person who would be picking her up. Serena desperately needed a bathroom break; the discomfort was making her tense, but she was afraid to leave the place where she was instructed to wait. Ten minutes passed, and people were meandering back and forth as she debated whether to race to the restroom on the opposite side of the terminal. The discomfort now unbearable, she began to pace. Then someone tapped her on the shoulder, startling her, she spun around. "Senora, Serena?

I am here for you." The man didn't smile or introduce himself.

"Can I please use the restroom first?"

"Yes, but be quick." He looked around suspiciously.

Soon, she was following him out of the terminal into the street, through a maze of people, vendors and fruit stands. They walked down a side street which led to a parking lot. The man approached a yellow, rust covered Volkswagen van that looked like it should be in its final resting place in a junk yard. When he put the key in the ignition, the engine coughed several times, jerking the van forcefully before it finally turned on.

They rode in silence through the busy streets; the driver looked straight ahead his expression intense, he appeared to be anxious about time. She stole glances at him. His face and well toned arms were sun burnt, reddish brown. He reminded her of the rugged look of the man in the Marlboro advertisement. Once, when he caught her looking at him, he said, "My name is Carlos. I am taking you to the house." Serena smiled and looked away.

The house was a small four-room cement structure where a short, plump, middle-aged woman greeted her at the door and pulled her inside. She heard Carlos drive away as the door closed behind her. "Come, Senora, sit. I fix you something to eat." The woman waddled off in the direction of the kitchen, her long, straight black hair draping almost past her buttocks. Serena sat on the sofa and looked around the room; there was a young man asleep on the floor in one corner of the room snoring softly. The room was clean, sparsely furnished, with pictures of Jesus on the cross and the Virgin Mary, affixed to the walls with tape. The 12-inch black and white television was on with a western movie in progress. When the woman reappeared with a plate in one hand and a glass of juice in the other, she nodded toward the man asleep on the floor and whispered, "He tired, he from Honduras, took him four days."

Serena ate the hot tacos, and before long she also fell asleep sitting on the sofa with the empty plate in her lap. Sometime later, she was startled by the sound of a door closing. When she opened her eyes, it was dark outside. A small lamp light the room and she saw that two more men and a woman with a baby had arrived. Carlos had come into the house; he spoke briefly with the woman, and then left with their bags of personal belongings, including the money they were traveling with. Shortly after, another man came in; he was tall and muscular with the compelling presence of a leader. He introduced himself as Miguel and announced that he would be taking them across. Later that night, the small group who had stayed briefly at Juanita's home, followed him quietly to a van that took them to an isolated spot on the bank of a river where the second part of their journey began together.

Chapter 2

There was a soft knock on the door, and a voice said, "Senoras, please, it's time to wake up to get ready." Serena forced herself to sit up from the narrow space she occupied on the bed. She had slept for less than two hours after a difficult time falling asleep.

"Do you want to use the bathroom first?" Teresita asked, yawning and rising slowly.

"No, you go ahead," Serena replied, allowing her body to fall back onto the bed.

The baby next to her made a grunting sound, stretched his legs and moved his arms. Serena sat up, reached over and picked him up, cuddling him. His lips began to move with anticipation and his eyes tried to focus on her face. When Teresita came back into the bedroom she was dressed. She smiled at Serena cuddling her son and whispering to him. "I'll get his bottle ready," she said, opening a can of formula and filling two baby bottles, one of which she took into the bathroom, and placed it under running hot water. "Come here, mi amore," she said reaching for her baby. Serena kissed the baby on the forehead before handing him to Teresita.

On her way to the bathroom, Serena still drowsy almost tripped over the garbage bag that contained all of their wet clothing from the night before; Miguel had told them that everything they wore would be thrown away. While washing and getting dressed in the bathroom, she heard soft laughter and joyful sounds coming from the bedroom. A few minutes later when she opened the bedroom door, Teresita and a man were locked in embrace, both crying and whispering to each other. It was Juan! Teresita's husband. He lifted her off the floor and spun her around. Tears of joy rolled down their cheeks. As he tenderly put her down, they stared at each other for a moment before their lips met in a passionate and loving kiss. Serena closed the bedroom door and went back into the bathroom to be alone for a moment, as her eyes flooded with tears, anticipating her own reunion with Nick.

Teresita and Juan were the first to leave the apartment early that morning. Shortly after they left there was a soft knock on the door. A short, skinny young man wearing a white cowboy hat and tight jeans tucked into his black cowboy boots entered the apartment. His face lit up when he embraced Roberto and Luis; he spoke briefly with Miguel, shook his hand and the two men left with him. Serena and Jose were the last to leave that morning; they were heading in the same direction. The driver of the white van from the night before returned, and Miguel accompanied Serena and Jose to San Diego's International Airport for their 11.00 a.m. flight to Chicago. On the way, he gave them instructions on how to act and what to say if they were questioned. He reassured them that since they were flying within the United States, there was no need for documentation, "It would be easy," he said, and it was. They presented their tickets at the airline counter; the attendant tapped the keys on the keyboard, looked at the computer screen for a moment, then handed them their boarding passes. They were seated next to each other on the flight to Chicago, and also on the connecting flight to New York City. The gentle rocking of the plane and the humming of the engine lulled Serena to sleep almost immediately after the plane took off.

She began to dream. She was sitting on the front porch steps, watching amusedly as Benny followed a hen and her six yellow baby chicks around the yard. He tried repeatedly to pick up one of the chicks, but each time it ran off before he could close his hands around it. She smiled at his persistence and lack of fear of the hen, which looked at him, straightened her neck and spread her wings apart clucking angrily.

She was startled and awakened by the pressure on her forearm. It was Jose trying to wake her as the flight attendant stood in the aisle next to them offering a meal on a tray. She smiled, "Thank you." Shortly after, another flight attendant offered them head sets for the in-flight movie. Jose purchased two headsets and handed one to Serena. The movie was Grease, portraying the American high school culture, so very different from her own.

Two hours later, the plane began its descent to New York's JFK International Airport; the pilot announced that it was 70 degrees and raining. After a slight bump, the plane taxied down the runway to the terminal, Serena stared out the window at the fleeting images and began to feel anxious. She had finally made it to America! She would find Nick; he would be surprised, then happy that they were together again. Jose touched her arm to get her attention; she looked up and saw passengers forming the line to disembark the airplane. She gathered her possessions and fell in line, with Jose directly behind her.

As they walked through the terminal and down the escalator following the exit signs, Jose looked around anxiously. When they approached the main doors, a young woman waved her hands, gleefully jumping up and down. Jose practically knocked Serena over as he sprinted forward. He dropped his travel bag and scooped the smiling, young woman up into his arms. They kissed each other over and over, finally locking in the tightest embrace. This was the second intense reunion that Serena had witnessed that day and she smiled imagining her long-awaited reunion with Nick being this joyful.

Jose suddenly turned around and beckoned Serena to come. "I am sorry, Senora, this is my girlfriend, Louisa."

"Nice to meet you," Serena said extending her hand.

"Is your family here?" Jose asked with the look of concern on his face.

"A friend is picking me up," she looked around. "But she is not here yet."

Jose, hugging her, said, "Good luck with everything, Senora."

Smiling, Serena replied, "You, too. Thanks for everything." She watched them as they walked away with their arms around each other, and imagined them having a long, blissful life together.

Emma Francis was the young lady picking Serena up at the airport, and with whom she planned to spend a day or two until she made contact with Nick. They had never met, but had photographs of each other. Emma's mother was a longtime friend of Aunt Julia, and she volunteered her daughter who lived in Brooklyn to provide hospitality. Serena pulled out the photo of Emma and looked at it for a moment. She then made her way to the seats lining the wall of windows, sat and waited. As she sat there looking at the constant flow of people rushing back and forth, carrying children, pushing strollers, pulling luggage, she remembered how hopeless she felt six weeks ago, and now she was sitting in an airport in America.

❧ ❧

She had been denied a vacation visa at the American Embassy in Belize City, because according to the Consulate, she did not have enough reasons to return to Belize and was considered high risk for remaining illegally in the U.S. She was in tears as she walked away from the embassy to the bus depot. The next day she was hanging wet clothing to dry on the clothes line at the back of the house when her friend Valerie stopped by for a chat. Valerie noticed immediately that Serena was in a somber mood, and demanded to know what was wrong. Serena told her about the disappointing trip to the embassy, and her hope of reuniting with Nick now lost. Valerie, with her "take charge" personality, grabbed Serena's face firmly, looked into her tear-filled eyes and said, "If you want to go this badly, we'll find a way to make it happen." Two days later, Valerie stopped by and gave her information that rekindled her hope.

❧❧ ❧❧

She was so engaged with her thoughts that she did not see Emma approaching.

"Serena?" She looked up and noticed the young woman standing in front of her. "Sorry you had to wait. The traffic was terrible on the Belt Parkway." Emma declared warmly. Serena rose to her feet and they embraced. "That's okay, I haven't been waiting long."

The rain fell hard and the traffic out of the airport moved slowly. Emma looked over at Serena, she was visibly exhausted. "You must be very tired, just relax, we have plenty of time to talk later." Relieved that Emma was so thoughtful, Serena reclined the seat, closed her eyes and was soon in a state of tranquility as they made their way out of the airport to Brooklyn.

❧❧ ❧❧

Sirens blasted in the air, rudely startling Serena out of a deep sleep. It took her a few moments to remember where she was, and rolling to the middle of the bed she hugged the second pillow tightly; it felt good to be in a clean, warm bed. She was beginning to drift off to sleep again when the sound of another siren blared outside the bedroom window. Serena got out of bed and opened the vinyl window shade. She looked outside at the busy street below and was filled with a sense of excitement and anticipation. Emma had suggested resting that first day to prepare herself physically and emotionally to meet Nick.

The apartment was neat, and nicely furnished. Emma was doing well for herself, working at a prestigious bank in midtown Manhattan. During their dinner together, Serena learned that after graduating high school in Belize, Emma had received a scholarship to attend university in America. She earned a bachelor's degree in business administration and after graduating, applied to the Immigration and Naturalization Service, for a work permit under the F1 student visa optional, practical, training program. She was granted a visa for two years to work in her field of study. As the end of the second year was approaching, Emma was in the process of applying for permanent residence status. She was attending graduate school at night, not dating, and was content with her life.

Serena ate a simple breakfast of toast with butter and jam and orange juice, then sat on the sofa in the living room to write a letter to her aunt. She paused for a moment wondering how her son was handling her absence. Trying hard not to feel any guilt about leaving him, she reasoned that it was not possible to bring him along like Teresita had done with her baby. After writing briefly about the trip, Emma's hospitality, and expressing her gratitude to her aunt for taking care of Benny, Serena ended the letter by asking her aunt to convey to her friend Valerie that everything went well for her.

She smiled as she thought of her childhood friend Valerie, now a vivacious, funny, assertive young woman. She was a stark contrast to Serena's gentle spirit and laid-back personality. In elementary school, Valerie fought all Serena's battles; she was fearless even as a little girl. Whenever Serena was upset or disappointed she turned to Valerie who now worked at a local bank on Burns Avenue, and knew about everything in the community. When Nick's letters stopped coming, Valerie said, "Girl, sounds to me like he moved on to greener pastures." Serena quickly dismissed the comment, as Valerie being in a state of bitterness toward men because of her dramatic break-up with Antonio.

Antonio had a possessive personality, but he couldn't control Valerie, and that frustrated him. One morning he had come to the house where she lived with her parents. Valerie was washing clothes in a large outdoor tub in the back yard when a heated argument erupted between them. Hot tempered Antonio became angry and overturned the bucket with the clothes that Valerie had already washed onto the muddy ground and stomped on them. Valerie screamed at the sight of what he had done. Her anger escalated, she ran into her father's tool shed and grabbed hold of a machete.

With Valerie in pursuit cursing loudly and waving the machete, Antonio ran around the house and into the street where neighbors immediately became curious spectators. Valerie's mother ran out of the house and stood in the middle of the street, her head and arms raised up to the sky, she cried out, "Jesus, Mary and Joseph, stop this child from committing a serious crime here today!" Her prayer was answered. One neighbor described Antonio's flight as 'Speedy Gonzalez' and thankfully he escaped a painful encounter with the sharp edge of a machete. Valerie spent most of the morning crying and re-washing the clothes, while Serena helped and tried to console her.

The phone rang, startling Serena. It was Emma calling to see how she was.

Chapter 3

The next day, following the directions that Emma had given her, Serena stepped off the bus at the corner of Rockaway Parkway and East 94th Street. As she walked down East 94th, she looked at the numbers on the attached two-story brownstone houses on both sides of the street. It was a beautiful late afternoon, warm and sunny, a light breeze touching her bare shoulders. She wore a pink and white halter sun dress and white sandals. Her thick black hair was shinning and bouncing around her shoulders as she walked. That morning, she had stared at herself in the mirror after applying the make-up that Emma had given her, and felt like a princess preparing to meet her prince.

Nick should be home from work by now, she reasoned as she walked pass #182, where four little girls were playing on the sidewalk, two of them turning the ropes while the other two jumped and chanted something about a baby. They abruptly paused their skipping and stared at her as she walked by. Serena's anticipation increased. She was within yards of reuniting with the love of her life; she imagined the surprise, the joy, the excitement they would soon share just like Teresita and her husband and Jose and his girlfriend.

The house with the large brass numbers 178 on a bright red door had a well-kept front yard with yellow marigolds in large pots at the base of the steps. Serena opened the gate, climbed the six steps to the landing, and paused to take a deep breath before pressing the bell with the name "Garcia" written in small print next to it. Her heart began to race as she waited. She pressed the bell a second time and heard an inner door open, followed by someone shouting, "Coming, coming."

When the outer door opened, Serena was greeted by a young woman wearing an oversized white shirt over black cotton shorts. "Hi," the woman said, one hand on her hip and the other rubbing her huge belly.

Serena hesitated and then said, "I am sorry, I must have pressed the wrong bell. I am looking for Nick Garcia's apartment." She quickly looked at the bells again.

"This is Nick's apartment," the woman declared. "I'm his wife."

Serena's gaze locked on the woman's face, and as her mind processed what she heard, her body became paralyzed. It was as if all the oxygen had been sucked out of her.

"Are you a friend of Nick's, from Belize?" the woman asked. Serena could not speak, or move, and was about to crumble into a lump of lifeless flesh on the landing, but the woman reached forward and offered her hands. Serena slumped against her.

"Are you okay?" she asked.

Serena covered her mouth with one hand and held onto the door frame with the other. After a moment, she whispered, "I feel dizzy."

The woman, supporting her by the arm, said, "Come inside, I'll get you something cold to drink."

Serena allowed the woman to lead her into the apartment to a chair at the dining table where she collapsed and covered her face with both hands. She was beginning to feel a wave of nausea like she had never felt before, not even during the months of morning sickness when she was pregnant with Benjamin.

"Here, drink this, it's lemonade," the woman offered. "You'll feel better."

With the first sip of the lemonade, her tongue became unglued from the roof of her mouth. So she took a deep breath and drank half of the lemonade before setting the glass down and staring at the woman sitting across from her.

"How do you feel now?"

Serena forced a smile, "Thanks for the lemonade."

There was an uncomfortable silence until the woman spoke, "So, you are visiting from Belize? I hear it is a beautiful country. I can't wait to go with Nick to visit his grandmother, when the baby is older of course. I am due to deliver in two weeks. My doctor put me on bed rest last week; by the way, my name is Sheila." Serena nodded and forced a smile. Sheila looked down at her belly and continued, "I can't believe I am going to be a mother," she said, rubbing her belly again. "Everything happened so quickly."

"What do you mean?" Serena asked, trying desperately to hide the pain and disappointment that was mounting after every word the woman shared.

"Well, we've only been married 12 months. I knew Nick for about six weeks before we got married. He used to work with my cousin, Ray, who set us up. It was supposed to be an arrangement, you know… Nick pays me some money, we get married and I sponsor him as my husband to get his green card, then later we divorce." She smiled and shrugged her shoulders. Serena could not believe how casual she was about this act of deception. Sheila continued, "But then it became for real. He is a real nice guy, and a good man is hard to find. I've had my share of losers, so I wasn't going to let this one get away. We are happy, especially having a baby together."

Serena closed her eyes and took a deep breath. Sheila was concerned again. "Are you still feeling dizzy?"

"I'm feeling better," she lied.

Sheila got up from the table and moved around the kitchen. She was a beautiful Hispanic woman, with olive tone skin, and soft feminine features. The joy of impending motherhood was visible in the glow that permeated her face. She carried her large round belly well on her tall frame, as she moved gracefully around in the kitchen. She appeared to be in a place of emotional contentment, and why shouldn't she be? Serena thought. Sheila had no idea of the promises

Nick had made to her, and that he had a son. Judging from the neat and nicely decorated apartment, Sheila was obviously a good housekeeper, wife and soon-to-be mother. But Serena could not endure hearing more disturbing details of Nick's happy life with her. She needed to be alone to cry, to let out the tears she was holding back, that would gush like a waterfall if she continued to sit at the table listening to Sheila.

She rose slowly from her seat and said, "I am sorry I missed Nick, but I should go now; I am not feeling very well."

Sheila was genuinely concerned. "Are you sure you don't want to rest a little longer?"

Serena shook her head. "No, I should be getting back now."

Sheila went to the refrigerator to get a small bottle of water for Serena. "I don't know what's keeping him, he's usually home by now." As they walked to the door, she added, "You didn't tell me your name."

Serena thought for a minute, then said, "Tell Nick that Serena came to see him, and that Benny sends his love."

Sheila quickly looked for a pen and paper, "I'll give you our phone number, please call him to arrange a visit before you go back to Belize." She handed Serena the piece of paper, smiled and said, "It was nice meeting you."

"Nice meeting you, too," Serena said, her chin dropping, afraid that if she looked at Sheila's face she would burst into tears.

As soon as the door closed behind her, the tears flowed unceasingly. She was halfway down the block from #178 when she turned back just in time to see Nick bouncing up the stairs and letting himself into the front door.

❀❧ ❧❀

The bus was not crowded; she was able to get a seat by herself next to the window, but the scenes outside the window did not register in her vision or mind; instead, she saw memories of her life with Nick playing like a motion picture.

Serena had met Nick during her senior year in high school, while living in Belize City and attending St. Catherine's Academy High School for Girls. The family, who had employed her mother as their Nanny before her tragic death, lived and owned retail businesses in the city. When Serena started attending high school, they allowed her to live with them during the week, and she went home to San Ignacio on the weekends. It was during her high school years that Serena discovered the joy of reading romance novels; her favorite author was Barbara Cartland. The heroes in the stories were always men who were strong, courageous, tall, dark and handsome. That was the kind of man she fell in love with and happily married in her daydreams. The high school boys she met did not measure up to the images in her mind, then one day she saw Nick.

He was an auto mechanic in a repair shop on Regent Street. The first time their eyes met, she was walking pass the shop, Nick flashed his charming smile, and it didn't matter that his blue overalls were dirty and stained with engine oil; he was indeed, tall, dark and handsome. From that day forward, she walked down Regent Street almost every day after school. Serena loved the feeling in the pit of her stomach when she felt his eyes on her, and the way her heart would race as she walked by slowly and with deliberate poise. Her fantasies staring Nick would rival the best of Barbara Cartland's romances.

One day, as she was walking by, Nick rolled out from underneath a truck in the driveway of the shop, stood up, trotted a few steps and fell into pace with her. As he walked along beside her, he told her she was beautiful, and made her smile when he said that heaven must be missing an angel. Suddenly, Serena's face had the sensation of being hot, her mind became muddled and she couldn't speak. She allowed him to do the talking in that first close encounter. After that day, it became difficult for her to focus on school work; she daydreamed about Nick and was becoming more and more intoxicated by his charm, and weak in the knees at the intensity of his gaze when he looked at her. Serena missed classes, lied to her teachers and her host family, she also made excuses to remain in the city on the weekends.

At the end of the second marking period her senior year, Serena was summoned to the office by her science teacher Mrs. Clark, who expressed concern that her grades were reflecting a lack of commitment and warned her that she might not meet graduation requirements. But spending time with Nick and creating her own love story was all that mattered to her. She managed to improve her grades just enough to graduate. The week of graduation she turned 17, and that same week Serena found out that she was pregnant.

Returning home to San Ignacio after graduation was hard. She agonized for days about telling her aunt and uncle, especially since Aunt Julia was eagerly suggesting to her different places to look for employment, or applying to the University to study nursing. Soon however, she began to feel guilty about the secrets and the lies; so on the morning that Aunt Julia asked how she was coming along with her resume, she confessed everything. Uncle George said nothing; he ate his breakfast and left to tend to the animals and his vegetable garden, but Aunt Julia made her disappointment known throughout that day, and during the weeks that followed.

The months leading up to the birth of Benjamin were difficult, but she was always happy when she was with Nick, who was finally allowed to visit her at the house, thanks to the intervention of her uncle. But she was constantly reminded by her aunt of the financial burden she had brought on herself and the family. When the baby was born, however, aunt Julia softened. She had never had children of her own and the baby seemed to fill the unspoken void she must have felt all those years.

Nick acted responsibly and soon had the admiration of her aunt and uncle. He chose the name Benjamin for his son because he said, "It means, son of my right hand." When Benjamin was three months old, Serena got a job at the San Ignacio Hotel as a receptionist; however, six months later she was laid off because of a slower than normal tourist season. It was shortly after she lost her job that Nick announced he was going to America to pave the way for a better life for them.

Initially, Serena was upset. She was contented with the life they had, all they needed, she reasoned, was to get married, find a place of their own, and live happily ever after. But with Nick so excited about this dream of a better life, she soon became attached to his excitement for their future. After he left, she tried to find another job close to home, but couldn't, so she settled into the routine of helping her uncle with his farm work and taking care of her son with financial support from Nick. When the letters stopped coming from Nick, her desire to be with him became more intense.

🍀 🍀

The bus jerked to a stop. Her eyes regained focus. Serena saw the familiar street and quickly got off, walking rapidly to the apartment. She paused before turning the key in the lock, hoping that this was a school night for Emma, because she needed time alone, to weep uninterrupted. But as soon as she pushed the door open, she heard, "Girl, what are you doing back here so soon? I thought for sure you would be gone for the night." Emma was in her bath robe, drying her hair with a towel. Serena did not answer. She leaned against the wall in the hallway and kicked her shoes off, she dropped her purse on the floor next to her shoes and without looking at Emma walked as if carrying a load on her shoulders over to the sofa and plopped down.

"Oh, no, what happened?" Emma asked.

"He's married, his wife is pregnant," was all she could mutter before bursting into tears. With her face buried in her hands, Serena sobbed, Emma looking helplessly at her.

For the remainder of the week Serena remained in the apartment, plagued by extreme sadness and uncertainty, feeling very helpless and vulnerable. She kept asking herself, "Now, what do I do?" Her dreams of a happy reunion were just that, dreams. The reality was a painful betrayal. She wallowed in self pity, sitting on the sofa keeping company with the crying women on the afternoon soap operas.

Chapter 4

E mma was compassionate during Serena's emotional melt-down; she allowed her time to grieve without saying too much, but still providing some comfort. During that time Serena began to admire Emma's strength and confidence, and wished she could be like her. Emma had definite goals for her life. She worked full time and attended New York University three nights a week, working on her MBA. Her priority was to develop herself first, to do the things she wanted to do, and if love found her on her journey, she would be ready.

By Saturday morning, Emma decided to do something to help Serena put aside the self pity and become proactive about her life. She knocked on the bedroom door. "I'm going to Flatbush Avenue. I'd like you to come with me. Maybe we could see a movie, do some shopping." Serena forced herself out of the bed and got dressed.

They stopped for lunch at a fast food restaurant, where Emma talked to Serena about getting past the hurt, and to start looking for opportunities for her own future. She suggested a live-in job as a nanny or a housekeeper, where she could get sponsorship by an employer for permanent residency status. On Sunday, Emma went to the corner store and bought a newspaper. Together, they looked for employment agencies, advertisements for babysitting and domestic help. On Monday morning, closely following the directions Emma had given her, Serena took the bus and trains to upper Manhattan to a domestic employment agency.

Unlike the modern skyscrapers of glass and steel in Mid and Lower Manhattan, the buildings in this part of the city were older with gothic-like architectural details framing the outside walls and large windows. These older buildings were an ashy gray color; their paint had faded with time and was replaced by a coat of dust. The streets were narrower, with vehicles parked on both sides in every inch of space. Delivery trucks lined up in the middle of the street, much to the annoyance of the motorists waiting behind them. The sporadic honking and shouting between motorists added to the noise and chaos as Serena walked from the subway, trying to locate her destination by looking at the numbers on the buildings. She was fascinated with the city; all the sounds and sights formed a rhythm to which everyone scurried.

After a 10 minute walk, she arrived at Building 438, the Jonah's Employment Agency. It took a moment for her eyes to adjust from the brightness outside to the poorly lit waiting room. The faded green carpet was dirty and worn in the walking path between the doorway and the receptionist desk. Black metal chairs, some with worn paint, lined both sides of the shabby room, and the smell of a burning cigar filled the air. The women sitting in the waiting area looked up as Serena entered. She looked around for a moment and then made her way toward the desk. A young woman appeared from behind the cubicle in the back of the room.

"May I help you?" She asked with a warm smile.

"Yes, I am looking for work as a live-in babysitter or housekeeper. I saw your ad in the newspaper."

"Will you be looking for sponsorship?"

"Yes ma'am."

The woman handed her a clipboard with an application already attached and said, "Complete this form and Mr. Jonah will discuss the process with you."

Serena felt all eyes on her as she sat down, away from the other women, to fill out the application. She heard a man speaking in an irritated voice behind the cubicle, where a cloud of smoke was rising to the ceiling.

"You were supposed to pay me at the end of your first week of employment," he shouted.

There was a pause, then he continued, "No later than Friday of this week, or I'll be forced to take action against you." He slammed the receiver violently. Some of the women snickered and looked at each other.

Serena turned her attention back to the form and realized she could not answer most of the questions, especially those that required information about previous employment and references. "Are you finished with the application?" The receptionist must have noticed her staring at the form. Serena sprang to her feet and handed the application to her. She glanced at it, looked up and said, "Mr. Jonah will see you now."

Mr. Jonah was writing vigorously on a note pad splattered with dry coffee stains. He motioned for her to sit, and then was suddenly overcome by convulsive coughing that turned his face beet red. When the coughing stopped, he cleared his throat and took a sip of coffee. Mr. Jonah had a disheveled appearance, wearing a wrinkled grey suit about two sizes too small. The open jacket revealed a dingy white shirt with buttons barely holding on because of his big, round belly. His face was unshaven, and the 12 strands of hair he fashioned into a comb-over on his bald head stayed neatly in place as if glued to his scalp. The desk was cluttered with papers, empty Styrofoam cups, pages of *The New York Times*, and a large rolodex. Mr. Jonah was sitting in front of a fire hazard, with a burning cigar and overflowing ashtray amidst the clutter. He looked at Serena from above the rim of his glasses, and without smiling he asked, "How old are you?"

"I'm 20," she said, sitting upright to appear taller.

He continued to stare at her. "Any experience with kids?"

"Yes sir, I have a 2-year-old son."

"Have you signed up with any other employment agency?"

"No sir."

He settled back in his chair. "Well, let me explain the process. I get calls daily from mothers and wives in the five boroughs, Westchester, Connecticut and New Jersey. They are looking for honest, reliable babysitters and housekeepers to provide live-in help. With most of the live-in positions, the families are willing to sponsor the employee to get their green card, that is, if they like the individual and things are going well. The benefit to the family is consistency for two to three years; that is about the length of time the green card process takes." He paused, crossed his forearms over his belly, and said as an aside, "When the time comes, I can give you the name of a lawyer who specializes in immigration cases." He cleared his throat, took a sip of coffee and continued, "My fee is the equivalent of one week's pay from you, and the same amount from your employer. I will schedule the interviews, and give you directions for the trains and buses. The prospective employer will pick you up at the train or bus station, take you to their home, and explain their expectations. If all goes well, you'll both agree on salary, starting date and scheduled days off. Do not accept a job unless it feels right for you." He leaned forward on the desk and stared at her above the rim of his glasses, "Any questions?"

"No sir." She shook her head, her eyes burning from the cloud of cigar smoke hovering around her.

"Well, I'll look at the requests I've gotten over the past few days, make some phone calls and we'll see what happens." He smiled for the first time. "Wait with the others and I'll call you in when I have something."

Serena sat away from the other women and waited. The air was stuffy as the smoke from Mr. Jones's cigar continued to rise above the walls of his cubicle and permeate the small waiting room. She stepped outside for a breath of fresh air. A woman was leaning against the building just a few feet from the doorway. Her head was down, but Serena recognized her as one of the women from the waiting room; she appeared to be crying softly. Serena walked over to her, reached into her purse for a tissue and handed it to the woman.

"Thank you," she whispered, staring straight ahead. After a moment, she turned to Serena and said, "I'm very upset that I have to start the process again."

"What do you mean?" Serena was confused.

"Well, I was a housekeeper for a family in New Jersey for over a year, they agreed to sponsor me, but when the INS sent some documents that the employer must complete, the woman refused."

Serena detected a West Indian accent, but she couldn't determine which island.

"Why did she refuse?"

"The INS requested a copy of their income tax return and other financial information; she refused to disclose their financial information."

The woman began to cry again. Serena's eyes filled up with tears, which always happened when she watched someone else crying.

"I can't believe this has happened to me," the woman said looking up toward the sky. "Things were going so well. I am anxious to get the green card, I want to go home to see my mother, it's been almost two years since I left home." She covered her face with her hands.

The opening of the door interrupted them. "Mr. Jonah is ready to speak with you Ms. Miller," the receptionist announced.

Serena put her hand on the woman's shoulder and whispered, "I am so sorry this has happened to you." She followed the receptionist back to Mr. Jonah's cubicle.

Mr. Jonah studied an index card, then looked up at Serena over the rim of his glasses. He shook his head and murmured, "No." Then looking at the card again, he said, "This could have been a possibility, but you are too attractive, this employer is specifically requesting someone who is homely."

"Homely?" She had never heard that word before.

"Well, she wants someone who is older, mature, and plain. She claims that her last housekeeper was young and very pretty. She felt that her husband flirted with the girl, which made her very uncomfortable. Although they desperately need the help, it's not easy for some women to have another woman living in their home."

Serena looked down at her hands and contemplated what he said, as he studied another index card. After about a minute of silence, Mr. Jonah said, "Okay, here is something." He looked at her, then at the index card. "This family lives in Englewood, New Jersey. They have two boys, ages three and five. I placed a woman there before, but after three weeks, she quit because the kids were too much for her. She was a much older woman though, I'm sure you could handle two rambunctious little boys. What do you think?" He did not wait for her answer, he dialed the phone number.

"Mrs. Kaplan, this is Mr. Jonah, how are you? Good, Good. I have a young lady who may be just perfect for your family." There was a pause. "You could see her today, wonderful." He looked up and winked at Serena. He scribbled vigorously on another index card. "Great, thank you, goodbye." He continued to write after placing the receiver on the cradle. "Now listen carefully," he said finally, giving her the index card. "Take the number seven train to the Port Authority bus terminal. Look for the New Jersey transit bus ticket counters, and purchase round trip tickets for the #23 bus going to Englewood. Ask the ticket agent for a bus schedule and the gate number. Call Mrs. Kaplan collect from a pay phone at the bus terminal to let her know what time the bus is scheduled to arrive on Bergen Street. She will be waiting to pick you up at the bus stop."

Serena left Mr. Jonah's Agency, followed his directions precisely, and was soon on a bus to New Jersey. The ticket agent told her that it was a 45 minute ride from Manhattan to Englewood, via the George Washington Bridge. She stared out the window in awe at the scenic wonder of the Hudson River, she had never seen a river so immense, and a bridge so magnificent. When she began to see signs for Englewood, her thoughts went back to earlier at the Employment agency where she had overhead some of the women describe their previous employers as harsh, condescending and inconsiderate. She hoped that Mrs. Kaplan was kind.

Soon, she was standing on Bergen Street, watching anxiously as the bus drove away, feeling as if she had been dropped off on a strange island. The afternoon sunlight was hot and blinding as she squinted looking up and down the busy shop-lined street.

Directly across the street from where she was standing, a woman got out of a car and waved her hands. "Serena?"

Serena waved back and ran across the street to her. They shook hands and exchanged greetings; Mrs. Kaplan opened the passenger door for Serena, and then hurried around to the driver's side. She looked in the rear view mirror and pointed to the back seat. "That's Zachary; he falls asleep as soon as he gets into the car." Serena looked at the sleeping child and smiled.

"You look very young, how old are you?" Mrs. Kaplan asked as she pulled out of the parking space. This was the second time today she was asked her age.

Serena smiled, "I'm 20."

"You look even younger. I'm 32, and I look 32," Mrs. Kaplan laughed. "By the way, I'd prefer if you called me Laura."

Laura Kaplan was tall and slender, with straight blonde hair draping her shoulders. She smiled a lot as she talked and gestured with her hands, sometimes taking both hands off the steering wheel. She spoke with ease about her family, and her struggle to choose between her career and being a stay at home mom. She seemed authentic, and as Serena listened and glanced occasionally at her, she felt at ease. Laura pulled into the driveway of a white split-level home on a quiet street of similar style homes, and large mature trees lining both sides of the street. She gently removed her sleeping child from the back seat. She whispered, "I don't want to wake him; he'll be cranky."

Serena followed her into the house and waited in the living room while she took Zachary upstairs to put him in his bed. When she returned, Laura took Serena to the basement to show her the living space. "It's a nice size bedroom," She said, as she opened a door adjacent to the laundry room. A full size bed and a large dresser drawer took up most of the space in the room, and a full bathroom was attached. "My mother-in-law lived with us for a while after my father-in-law passed a few years ago, but now this room is for live-in help."

"It's nice…. cozy," Serena said as they headed back upstairs.

In the kitchen, Laura prepared small tuna sandwiches while she explained her expectations. As they sat across from each other at the dinette table, she asked Serena some personal questions and didn't seem too concerned about Serena's limited experience with child care and housekeeping. So Laura Kaplan offered her the job at $120 a week to start, and was willing to be her sponsor for permanent residency.

"I have to be honest with you, though," Laura said, her gaze suddenly downcast. "The boys are challenging, but not unmanageable with the right person taking care of them. My mother took care of them before she remarried and moved to North Carolina about a year ago. Since then, we have been relying on live-in help, which never seems to work out." She paused and looked out the window, "My husband and I disagree on the subject of my working. He wants me to stay at home, but I want to work."

She reached and touched Serena's hand across the table. "I really hope this works out for us and for you too." She squeezed her hand gently and continued, "Think it over tonight, call me tomorrow morning, I would like you to start tomorrow evening if possible."

"I will," Serena replied, knowing already she would accept the job.

"Good, I am off for a couple days; I can get you settled in with the boys."

They decided on a work schedule beginning Sunday evenings and ending Friday evenings. In addition to her weekly pay, round trip bus fare would be provided. Laura Kaplan appeared to be pleased with their arrangement as she drove Serena back to the bus stop on Bergen Street, with Zachary awake, but quiet in the back seat.

Chapter 5

Serena's first meeting with Dave Kaplan, Laura's husband, was intimidating. It was in the evening, a few hours after she had arrived on the first day. He walked in the front door, shouted, "I'm home!" then headed upstairs. A few minutes later, he came into the kitchen dressed in running clothes, as Laura was explaining to Serena the strict nutritional meal plan for the boys, who were not allowed any snacks or drinks with sugar, and no dairy products.

"Dave, this is Serena, the new nanny," she made the introduction without looking at her husband. Dave looked at Serena, who found his facial expression intense.

"Hi," he said without enthusiasm, gathering items from the refrigerator to make a sandwich. His indifference was apparent, and after placing his sandwich on a plate, he headed for the living room.

Laura left the kitchen and went upstairs to look after the boys. Serena, who had barely interacted with them in the few hours she had been there, remained in the kitchen, opening cabinets to familiarize herself with its contents. Dave returned to the kitchen, opening the refrigerator again, he took a bottle of water, opened it and leaned against the countertop. He glanced at Serena for a moment, "So, do you have any experience working with children who have behavioral problems?"

"No, I don't." She looked at him puzzled by the question.

He sighed while shaking his head. Silence filled the kitchen. Serena felt knots in her stomach.

"What kinds of behavioral problems?" she asked curiously.

"Well, Josh, the oldest, is autistic. He is unable to speak, probably never will, who knows." He shrugged his shoulders, continuing to explain, "Zachary, the 3-year-old, may also be on the spectrum, he hasn't been diagnosed yet, but he is definitely showing the signs." He stared ahead with a blank look on his face. After a long uncomfortable pause, he continued, "What this means is that they have very difficult behaviors that will frustrate you. We have tried Nannies before, but have been unable to keep them. My wife insists on working, even though she doesn't have to. I want her to stay home and care for the boys, so pardon me if I do not seem excited that you are here. I told Laura that I am willing to try this one final time. She's promised me if it does not work out this time, she will quit her job." He smiled half-heartedly and left the kitchen. Serena heard the front door close behind him.

That night as she lay in bed in the basement bedroom, Serena worried about impressing the Kaplans, and wondered if she could handle the job, since Dave Kaplan had planted the seed of doubt in her mind. She woke up at 6 a.m., showered, dressed and was upstairs in the kitchen at 6:45, where the smell of coffee greeted her; she noticed that the coffeemaker had been started. Laura came downstairs shortly after 7:00, she appeared to be dressed for work. "Good morning, did you sleep well?" She asked as she filled a travel mug with steaming coffee. Serena was confused; Laura had told her that she would be at home for at least a day to help her and the boys with the transition. Now, she was pointing to the refrigerator. "That index card has my work number on it; call me if you need help with anything."

She left the kitchen, Serena followed, wanting to ask questions, but Laura moved quickly as if trying to escape. As she was putting on her jacket, she added, "Oh, I almost forgot to tell you, the bus picks Joshua up at 8:15." She was at the front door now. "Wake him up about 7:20; it takes him a long time to eat breakfast. Let Zach sleep for as long as he wants to, don't wake him up." She opened the door and stepped outside. "I'll be home between 5.00 and 5:30. Dave usually gets home later than me. Just call me if you have any questions."

"Bye," was all Serena had a chance to say as Laura quickly closed the door behind her.

Waking Joshua was more difficult that she had imagined. He became irritable as she walked him to the bathroom. He refused to brush his teeth, and would not allow her to help him or wash his face. He kept resisting, screaming, attempting to bite her hands. She closed the bathroom door so the screaming would not wake Zachary, and tried desperately to comfort Joshua. "It's Okay Josh." Serena knelt down and put her arms around him, but he pushed against her, arched his back and when she let him go he crawled to the corner where he sat screaming repeatedly, "No!" After waiting helplessly for five minutes, staring at the screaming child, she left the bathroom.

She returned a few seconds later with the blanket and the brown teddy bear he had been clutching while he was asleep. She handed them to him; he immediately squeezed them against his chest, and started to rock back and forth. Serena sat on the floor next to him and gently rubbed his back. He stopped rocking, gave her a momentary glance, and then covered his head with the blanket. She waited. It was 7:45. Not knowing what to do next, she said, "The school bus is coming!" Joshua pulled the blanket off his head and stood up suddenly.

"Let's get ready for the school bus," Serena added in a singing tone.

He was suddenly cooperative; allowing her to wash and dress him, then followed her downstairs with his blanket in one hand and brown bear in the other. He drank the warm vanilla flavored almond milk, but had no interest in the waffle and sausage on the plate. He tightened his lips and turned his head when she tried to feed him.

The bus arrived promptly at 8:15. Serena helped Joshua up the three steps. The bus driver, a man with graying hair and beard, smiled and asked, "You the new babysitter?"

"Yes, today is my first day."

He chuckled, winked one eye and said, "Well, good luck honey," as he closed the doors. She stood on the curb and watched as the bus drove noisily down the street, and wondered why the bus driver was so cynical.

Back in the house, Serena sat at the kitchen table, looking at the list of things that had to be done. Yesterday, Laura had said she was behind with the laundry and that was priority. Before heading to the laundry room in the basement, Serena went upstairs to check on Zachary. He was not asleep in his bed. She called his name repeatedly, looking in the bathroom, the guest bedroom and finally his parent's bathroom. What she found made her frantic. Zachary had taken off his soiled diaper and the floor was wet with urine. He had an open bottle of lotion in his hand, which he had rubbed in his hair and over his face. She spent the next hour bathing and dressing Zachary, and cleaning the mess he had made in the bathroom. By evening on that first day when she retired to her bedroom in the basement, Serena was exhausted from the hectic pace of the day.

Each morning she faced a battle of the wills waking Joshua and getting him ready for school. He was easily frustrated, piercing Serena's ears with his violent screams, and resisting her touch. What calmed him one day, irritated him the next; but she was patient. After Joshua left for school, she faced another challenge, keeping Zachary safe. He was fearless, often climbing onto high surfaces, including the window sills. He was not an independent or trustworthy child who could be left alone to play with toys or watch television. His attention span was extremely short and he was in constant motion. She found it difficult to get the required housework done with ease, because Zachary required constant supervision.

At the end of each day, Serena was thoroughly exhausted from trying to keep up with the housework and physical demands of taking care of the boys. She noticed the brothers didn't play together; they each seemed to be in their own world, oblivious of the other except when they fought over toys. When Laura asked how things were going, Serena always smiled and answered, "Everything is fine." However, the look on Dave's face told her that she wasn't fooling him. By the end of her first week, she was beginning to doubt her ability to do the job. "Maybe it will become easier as you develop a routine and the boys get to know you better," Emma said, when Serena expressed her doubts.

But things did not improve in her second week. She tried waking Joshua earlier to give him more time for his meltdown, recovery and breakfast, but it was becoming a difficult way to start her day. She tried to keep Zach close to her as she did the housework, but he was afraid of the sounds from the dishwasher, vacuum, and washing machine. He would run out of the room covering his ears, screaming. The difficulty of trying to complete the housework and dealing with the boys' abnormal behaviors was getting her down; she left for Brooklyn that second weekend less hopeful that things would become easier.

At the beginning of her third week, Serena asked Laura for large containers to organize the toys. Zachary loved his collection of small cars; there were at least 50 in his container. Arranging his cars in a straight line was the longest he remained in one spot. As she started the housework on Tuesday morning, Serena gave him his container of cars to play with on the living room floor; she hoped that would keep him occupied for awhile. She went upstairs to make the beds and clean the bathrooms. About 10 minutes later, she crept quietly down the stairs to check on Zachary. He was still taking the cars out, one at a time, and meticulously lining them up neatly on the floor while babbling to himself. Serena hoped she could complete the upstairs chores before he lost interest in his cars.

She had made the beds and cleaned the boys bathrooms and was about to start on the master bathroom, but decided to check on Zachary again. Peering down into the living room from the top of the stairs, she saw that the cars were in a straight line, but Zachary was nowhere near them. Serena ran down the stairs calling his name. She felt a cool breeze and looked in horror at the open front door. She fled the house, still calling his name. He was not in the front yard. She began to panic, as horrible thoughts invaded her mind. She ran to the backyard, but there was no sign of Zachary. The next door neighbor was getting into her car in her driveway as Serena came from the back of the house. "Excuse me, have you seen Zachary?"

"No." The neighbor looked puzzled. "Did he get out of the house by himself?"

"Yes, I was upstairs for a few minutes. I left him in the living room playing with his cars, when I came down to check on him he was not there and the front door was open." Her heart was pounding against the wall of her chest as fear and anxiety took over her mind and body.

"I'll help you look for him," the neighbor declared. She locked her car and suggested they go in opposite directions on the street. It was mid-morning and no one was around on the quiet street. Serena quickened her pace, yelling for Zachary, looking on both sides of the tree-lined street, and looking back several times to see if the neighbor had found him. She walked quickly pass houses with well landscaped front yards and empty driveways. She was approaching the cul de sac, where the homes were on larger lots, some with privacy fences around the back yard. In desperation, Serena was about to head into one of the back yards where she noticed the gate was slightly open, but turned around frantically, and that's when she saw Zachary.

He was on the opposite side of the street, walking toward the front door of a house with a circular driveway, clutching one end of his blanket, the rest of it trailing behind him. Behind the fence a dog barked ferociously, but Zachary was undaunted by the sound. Serena ran across the street, dropped to her knees in front of Zachary, hugged him to her chest, relieved, she whispered, "Thank you, God... Thank you, God." But Zachary showed no emotion. He was not happy to see her; in fact, he looked past her, gazing off into the distance, babbling sounds. After a deep sigh of relief she got up, took the blanket from him, now dirty from being dragged along the ground, and he allowed her to hold his hand.

As they walked back to the house, Serena's body slowly released the tension and anxiety she felt over Zachary's brief disappearance. She debated in her mind whether or not to tell Laura what happened; she did not want to seem incompetent or give up too quickly. But how could she not say anything about the incident, when the neighbor who seemed relieved to see them walking up the street may talk to Laura about it. When Serena entered the house and watched in disbelief as Zachary effortlessly climbed the window sill of the bay window and stood with his face pressed against the glass, she came to the realization that she lacked the experience to take care of these two boys with such complex behaviors.

That evening, as Serena reported what had happened, Laura cried sadly. She conceded it was time for her to care of her sons. Her professional career, which she enjoyed so much, would have to be put on hold. The next morning, Dave wanted to speak with Serena before leaving for work. He had the look of "I told you so" on his face. He nicely stated that his wife had finally come to her senses, and it was what he always felt was best for the family. He asked Serena to remain until the end of the week, focusing only on the children.

Later, Laura came into the kitchen; her eyes looked as though she had been crying. She told Serena that she was comfortable with the decision. She would submit her letter of resignation immediately and use her two weeks of vacation. Serena suggested hiring someone to help with the house cleaning and laundry once a week, to give her more time to focus on the demands of the boys. Laura agreed that it was a good idea and she would consider it.

The remainder of the week was not without difficulties. On Thursday afternoon Joshua fell asleep on the bus. When the Aide on the bus woke him to walk him off the bus, he had a major meltdown, and bit Serena's hand as she tried to get him into the house. That morning, Zachary had taken a bottle of chocolate syrup from the pantry which had been left open accidently. He opened it and poured it all over himself and the kitchen floor.

On the way to the bus stop that final Friday afternoon, Laura Kaplan looked over at Serena and said, "I have to admit that I was using work as an escape from my reality. The boys are my responsi-

bility; I probably couldn't pay someone enough to deal with the behaviors I was trying to get away from. Thank you so much for all you
did and being so patient with them." She handed her an envelope.
"I gave you an additional week's pay since the job ended so abruptly
for you. I hope you find something else soon. I'm so sorry it didn't
work out with us."

Serena smiled. "Thank you, I'm very sorry, too." She turned and
looked at the boys in the back seat. Zachary was asleep and Joshua
was staring out the window. He did not look at her when she called
his name to say goodbye.

Chapter 6

The beginning of the first week after leaving the job, Serena went shopping for Benjamin with the extra money Laura Kaplan had graciously given her. She packed the new clothes and toys in a box, wrote a letter to her aunt, enclosed a money order and mailed it to Belize. On Wednesday morning, she made another trip to the Jonah Employment agency. Mr. Jonah reassured her that it was typical for an individual to change several jobs before finding the right one. He reminded her that since the process of sponsorship took two or more years, being comfortable in the job and liking the family was important. He scheduled her next interview for Saturday morning with a family in Summit, New Jersey.

Jeff and Karen Hanson and their two children, Hallie and Connor, met her at the train station in downtown Summit. They included her in their Saturday morning routine, having brunch at the deli on Morris Avenue. Mrs. Hanson asked her a few general questions about herself, then told her about their family. Turning to look at her husband who was sitting next to her, she said, "Jeff is an emergency room physician at Overlook Hospital, so he is gone a lot..." she stroked the back of his head, the expression on her face said, *I am proud of him.* She continued, "I teach in the science department at Rutgers University in Newark."

Serena felt very comfortable with this family who appeared to be very laid-back. The children were calm, well behaved, and friendly. Hallie, who was six, asked questions about Belize, and wanted to know where it was on the map. Then, she announced that she missed her previous nanny. "I know sweetheart, but she had to leave because she missed her family," Karen said, reaching across the table and stroking Hallie's face. She explained that the nanny was an Au Pair from Germany who, after two years with them, decided to return home.

At the end of the meal at the deli, they took Serena back to their home, where she spent a couple of hours touring the house, playing with the children and discussing expectations of the job with Karen. By the time they took her back to the train station, Serena and the Hansons felt that they were right for each other. As the trained pulled away from the station, Serena looked out the window at quaint Summit, and felt good about the family she had just met.

❧❧ ❧❧

Time races quickly, Serena thought as she lay in bed one Saturday morning in the apartment she shared with Emma in Brooklyn. It was now 12 months since she had been working for Karen and Jeff Hanson, and things couldn't be better. After six months on the job, the attorney that Mr. Jonah had recommended submitted the first documents to the INS. Mrs. Hanson had advertised the job in the newspaper to establish the need for childcare/housekeeping. She then had to provide proof to the INS that no American citizen had applied for the position. This was the process used to justify hiring someone who was not a US citizen, and thus establishing her desire to be a sponsoring employer.

Everything was going well. Serena settled into a nice routine working for Karen and Jeff. They were not demanding, she had the freedom to pace herself with the housework and she enjoyed taking care of the children who were very polite and affectionate. She left for the weekend on Friday evening and returned to work on Monday morning. Although she liked being with the family, she also looked forward to her weekends in Brooklyn with Emma. They had fun together, becoming very close friends. On Sundays they attended church with one of Emma's co-workers, and Serena was working on forgiving Nick.

One Friday evening at the train station Serena met Marie, who was also a housekeeper for a family in Summit. They developed a friendship and eventually coordinated their times to ride the train together on Friday evenings to New York and the bus on Monday mornings to New Jersey. Serena learned that Marie had been a nurse in Haiti before coming to the U.S. on a vacation visa. She over-stayed the allotted time on her visa to seek sponsorship through house-keeping employment. Marie worked for a couple in their early 50's who she described as "strange people." They had no children and lived in a large Victorian style home with two German shepherds. Marie had taken the job because there were no children to take care of, and the couple was gone all day. They owned and operated a printing business on Broad Street in Newark. She was responsible for the cooking, laundry and general housework, which included taking care of the dogs.

Serena liked Marie, who initially was guarded with her personal life. After a few rides together, she opened up about her personal struggles. Her relatives in Haiti depended on her for financial support, but her weekly pay was inadequate to support her and them, she felt pressured. She had come to hate her job, but couldn't leave since her employers were sponsoring her, and although her attorney assured her that all the necessary papers had been submitted, Marie hated the process of waiting and wanted to be free. She never talked about friends or family in Queens, where she spent her weekends in a small basement apartment. As the months went by, Serena noticed that Marie, who was medium height and slender, was gaining weight.

One Monday morning, the buses travelling to New Jersey were delayed because of an accident on the New Jersey side of the Lincoln Tunnel. As they sat in the terminal and waited, Serena noticed that

Marie seemed very distracted, off in her own thoughts even as Serena was talking to her about the weekend.

"I am having a baby," she said suddenly, staring past Serena's face.

"Really?" Serena was surprised; Marie had never mentioned a boyfriend or a husband.

After a long pause, she looked at Serena with tears in her eyes and said, "I don't know what I am going to do. How will I take care of a baby and do a live-in job?"

"Maybe your boss will allow you to keep the baby with you on the job," Serena said, trying to be encouraging. Marie did not respond. "Or maybe you could send the baby to Haiti, to your mother."

As the weeks passed and Marie was closer to her due date, Serena observed that she was more and more melancholy and withdrawn. The last Monday they rode the bus together, Marie said very little, staring out the window, occasionally wiping her eyes with a ball of tissues.

It was about 3:30 p.m. on Tuesday; the day after she had last rode the bus with Marie. Serena was fixing a meal for the children when the phone rang; it was Marie. She was struggling to speak between sobs. She was at Overlook Hospital and wanted Serena to come as soon as possible; she desperately needed her help. She had delivered a baby girl at 9:30 Monday night; the baby came two weeks early.

"I can ask Karen to drive me to the hospital as soon as she gets in from work. I'll be there as soon as I can," she promised, and hung up the phone, puzzled why Marie was so upset, and her frantic phone call.

Karen walked into the house a little after 5:00 p.m. and announced that she was taking the kids to her friend Melanie's house in Scotch Plains for a quick visit.

"My friend Marie is at Overlook Hospital," Serena said, as Karen filled a glass with orange juice. Karen knew about the friendship between them.

"Oh! Did she have her baby?"

"Yes, she delivered a girl, last night. She called me around 3:30 crying hysterically. She didn't say what was wrong, but begged me to come to the hospital to help her."

"Help her, how?" Karen asked.

"I don't know." Serena cleared the dishes off the table and placed them in the dishwasher.

"That is strange," Karen replied. "Well, I can drop you off at the hospital on my way to Melanie's and pick you up on my way back."

On the way to the hospital, Karen stopped at a florist and picked up a small vase with flowers for Marie.

"I'll pick you up in a couple hours; wait for me at this main entrance," she said, as Serena got out of the car.

The first thing Serena noticed as she walked into the room was the generous amount of flowers around the empty bed nearest the window. There were small baskets and vases of yellow, red and white roses, vibrant colors in an otherwise plain room. Marie was lying in the bed near the entrance of the room, with her back to the door.

"Hi, Marie," Serena said softly and walked around the bed to face her. "How are you doing?"

Marie's eyes were red and her face was wet, obviously still crying, she forced a smile. Serena continued, "Karen sent you these flowers with her warm wishes." Marie's night stand was bare except for a box of tissues. Serena was glad that Karen was so thoughtful. "Your roommate got a lot of flowers; since leaving Belize, I have not seen so many roses in one place."

Marie dried her eyes and sat up in the bed. "She has a lot of visitors; I think this is her first baby." After a long pause, Serena broke the silence.

"So, how is the baby? You were so upset on the phone, you had me worried."

Marie grabbed Serena's hand, and whispered with urgency in her voice, "I need your help; they want me to leave the baby here in the hospital, to give up my rights as her mother, and give her up for adoption."

Serena was shocked to hear this. "Who would want you to do such a thing?"

Marie began to cry again. "My boss and his wife," she said as she reached for the box of tissues on the night stand.

A nurse walked in, pushing a bassinet with a baby and announced in a singing tone, "Someone is hungry, time for Mommy to try to breast feed again." She picked up the baby and placed her into Marie's outstretched arms. The nurse left and Marie's face beamed as she unwrapped the blanket. She stared at the face of her baby, then showed the baby to Serena.

"She's beautiful, Marie." Serena gasped, then exclaimed, "Marie, your baby is white; I didn't know you were dating a ......"

Marie interrupted her with a resounding "No!" After a long pause, she said, "I wasn't dating anyone." Now, Serena was really confused. She waited for Marie to continue. After another long pause, Marie looked up and said, "It's my boss." Serena stared at her in disbelief.

"Were you having an affair with your boss?"

Marie began to sob again.

"I'm sorry." Serena stood up and put her arms around Marie's shoulders, "I didn't mean to sound so accusing."

"No, I didn't have an affair with him; he came to my bedroom in the basement twice and forced himself on me. I resisted and threatened him, he laughed at me, and said that he would withdraw his sponsorship, and see to it that I never got a green card. I hated that man so much that I got sick to my stomach every Monday morning when I had to come to the job. I wanted to quit, but my family depends on me; life is very hard for them in Haiti. I am their only hope." She looked down at the baby, who continued to sleep. "When I found out that I was pregnant, I was afraid to say anything to them, but when I started to show, I told the wife. That night, I heard her crying and screaming at him. I heard him deny it. "*How do we know what that woman does on the weekends?*" But she kept repeating, "*Why would she lie about a thing like that?*" Finally, he admitted it when she threatened to leave that night. She was angry for weeks. It was a nightmare being there, I was so scared I barely slept at nights. One day, when she finally started speaking to me again, she told me that for many years she was sad that she couldn't have children. Then, in my fifth month they started demanding that I have an abortion. But I told them that I couldn't, it's against my Catholic faith."

Serena looked closely at the sleeping baby. She had very pale skin and thick, straight black hair. Marie continued. "I called the lawyer handling my immigration papers about the end of my sixth month when I felt like I would go insane if I had to be there indefinitely. He told me the final documents required by immigration had been submitted, and since I already had my interview, he estimated that in about two to three months I should be receiving my permanent residence documents in the mail; that's what kept me going."

"That's good news, Marie. When did you have your interview?"

"Don't you remember about six months ago I told you that I had an appointment at the INS office in Newark?"

"Oh Yes, I remember."

She paused as if reflecting. "It has been very difficult continuing to work with them these past few months." There was a long silence as both women seemed to be deep in their own thoughts.

"What plans did you make for the baby?" Serena asked.

"I was planning to send her to Haiti to my mother, as you suggested, until I had my own apartment and a job where I wasn't required to live in."

"But why would your boss want you to give the baby up for adoption?"

Marie took a deep breath and sighed, "I think the wife was holding out hope that the baby was fathered by someone else, and not her husband. When I went into labor last night, they brought me to this hospital. She stayed with me during the birth and when she saw the baby, she knew. They visited me after I was assigned to this room and told me that I couldn't bring the baby back to their home, that I was better off giving her up for adoption. They threatened to withdraw their sponsorship."

Tears began to sting Serena's eyes; she felt that this was such an injustice and didn't know what she could do. The baby began to stir; she opened and closed her eyes, and moved her lips.

"Please Serena, you have to help me; I can't give her up, what if I never have another child."

There was silence between the women as Marie positioned the baby to nurse. "I am having a lot of discomfort with breast feeding." The baby finally settled into a good position and she began to suck. As Serena looked at the baby and Marie she thought, *some people paid a high price for the privilege of living in this land of opportunity*, and she became overwhelmed with sadness as she realized that Marie was another causality of the desperate desire for a green card.

Marie broke the silence. "The doctor said everything is fine for the baby and me to be discharged tomorrow. My boss wants me to talk to the social worker in the morning about giving up the baby. They plan to pick me up in the afternoon. Please help me to keep my baby," she pleaded.

Serena left the room not knowing what she could do to help Marie. She stood on the curb away from the main entrance of the hospital and waited for Karen. It was 7:30 p.m., still light out, and visitors were beginning to leave the hospital. The evening was cool with a slow breeze that just lightly touched her face as she leaned against the wall. The weather would soon change to unbearable heat as the middle of June approached; this would be her second summer here. Memories of Benjamin as a baby replayed in her mind and made her smile; she couldn't imagine giving him up for anything in the world. In her last letter, Aunt Julia described some of the funny things he said, and his precocious nature. She was missing all that. At 7:50, Karen pulled up to the entrance of the hospital.

"So, how are things with Marie and the baby?" she asked.

"They are both fine." Serena fastened her seatbelt.

"So, why was she crying and asking for your help?"

Serena looked at the kids in the back seat and whispered to Karen, "I'll tell you when we get home."

Later, when the children were in bed, Karen and Serena sat across from each other at the kitchen table. Karen's facial expression changed from disbelief to anger as Serena described Marie's predicament. Then, she stood up and declared, "We have to help her; this is not the dark ages. Who do these people think they are, using and abusing that poor woman, and then to have the nerve to demand that she give up a child she carried for nine months?" She began to pace around the kitchen. "I have to call Melanie; she's an attorney, she'll tell us what to do." She left the kitchen and went up to her bedroom. Serena continued to sit at the kitchen table; her chamomile tea got cold. She reheated it in the microwave oven and sat waiting for Karen to return to the kitchen.

The phone rang; it startled Serena and brought her back to the moment. Shortly afterward, she heard Karen's footsteps coming down the stairs. She looked at the clock on the microwave; she had been sitting, waiting for 20 minutes. Karen came into the kitchen with the look of victory on her face. "I spoke with Melanie, then she called Marie at the hospital for some information; she just called me back with a plan. I have to take the day off tomorrow so we could pull this thing off."

Serena was on her way to her bedroom when she heard the front door close and Jeff's voice. Karen will no doubt be telling him Marie's story while he ate dinner. She had no idea what the plan was, but she went to bed that night pleased that she was involved in the fight to right one injustice in the world.

The next morning, Karen announced, "We will be going to the hospital to pick Marie up around noon. Melanie spoke with her again this morning. She should be ready to leave the hospital by then."

Marie was sitting in a wheelchair, just inside the main entrance, when they arrived. She had the baby in her arms, and a nurse stood next to her holding a small duffle bag. She looked happier today, smiling and thanking Karen who took the baby and placed her in a small car seat that she had installed earlier. As they were turning onto the street from the hospital's main entrance, Marie suddenly shouted, "That's them, they are coming to pick me up." Karen stopped the car and looked in the direction Marie was pointing.

"I would love to be a fly on the wall in that hospital room to see their reaction when they enter and find you and the baby gone."

When they arrived at the house, Karen asked Serena to share her bedroom with Marie and the baby. She gave them clean linens for the bed, and towels for Marie, then she headed to the basement. Connor stayed in the bedroom staring at the baby in the car seat; he seemed fascinated with the tiny infant. Half an hour later, Karen appeared in the bedroom with a bassinet, which she placed next to the bed; it already had clean bedding, a blanket and small pillow in it. She picked up the sleeping baby and placed her in the bassinet. "Look at her, she is so beautiful." The three women and the little boy stood around the bassinet staring at the sleeping infant.

Finally, Karen broke the silence. "I have had this bassinet since Hallie was born," she declared proudly as she touched the ruffles along its rim. "Marie, I have a box of baby clothes; some things are practically new." She left the bedroom and came back shortly with a bag. "I was saving these in my closet; you can have them. I also have some new baby bottles and a breast pump; you might want to pump some breast milk for later today." She began to leave, then turned and said to Connor, "Come on down with me, honey, I'll fix you some lunch." Connor shook his head, "No," and remained in the bedroom with the two women and the baby.

It was 4:30 in the afternoon when Jeff walked in. Serena was surprised that he was home so early, but when Karen announced to her and Marie that they were meeting Melanie at the Jacobson's home in 30 minutes, she understood why. Jeff was asked to be home early to take care of the children while Karen, Serena and Marie went on their mission. As the three of them prepared to leave, Karen said to him, "Honey, the baby is asleep, keep Connor away from her. If she wakes up, there is a bottle in the fridge; you know what to do."

Marie was visibly nervous. "Why are we going there?" she asked from the back seat.

"I don't know the details, but Melanie is a good attorney; she will be the one doing the talking, but she insisted that you should be there." Karen responded, looking at Marie through the rear view mirror.

They were at the Jacobson's driveway in less than 15 minutes. It was an impressive two-story, white Victorian home with large windows framed by green shutters. The house was on a large lot and was surrounded by tall, robust oak trees; the shrubs and grass were well manicured. There were two cars parked at the curb in front of the house, one of them was a police car. A very attractive young woman, dressed in a well-tailored 2 piece navy blue suit, was speaking with the police officer. Karen got out of the car first. She walked over to the pair, spoke with them briefly, and then returned to the car to get Marie and Serena. Marie's hands were shaking. "I really don't want to see them; I'm so scared."

Melanie walked over to Marie and offered her hand. "Hi Marie, I'm Melanie Richardson." She paused as she saw the tears welding up in Marie's eyes. She held Marie's hand firmly with both of hers and added, "Don't be scared, we are here to collect something that belongs to you." She beckoned to the police officer, "Let's go."

The police officer rang the doorbell, and the group behind him waited in silence. Serena was anxious to see the face of the man who used his position as employer to prey on someone in such a vulnerable situation. The man who opened the door had a bewildered looked on his face as he stared at the group standing at his door.

"Are you Mr. Jacobson?" the police officer asked, presenting his badge.

"Yes, what's this about?" He removed his glasses, his eyes scanning the faces looking back at him.

"I'm Officer O'Hagan and this is Mrs. Melanie Richardson, the attorney representing Ms. Du Bois," the officer stated calmly. There was no response from the man who was now staring at Marie, who kept her head down. The officer continued, "Mrs. Richardson is here to get something that is the property of her client." Mr. Jacobson remained speechless, but beads of sweat were forming on his forehead as he now appeared nervous.

The sound of footsteps was heading in their direction. The door opened wider and a short, stocky woman wearing a colorful sun dress, her face heavily made-up asked, "What's going on?" The officer stepped aside and Melanie stepped closer to the door.

"Mr. Jacobson, I spoke to Ms. Du Bois' immigration attorney this morning, he informed me that he was notified by INS in writing about four weeks ago that Ms. Du Bois' passport and green card were mailed to her at her employer's address. He also stated that he left two messages on your answering machine for Ms. Du Bois, requesting his final payment and there's been no return phone call." She paused, looking first at Mrs. Jacobson then at Mr. Jacobson; they both just stared back at her. "Mr. Jacobson, did you receive Ms. Du Bois' mail from the INS?"

The wife answered quickly before he could respond, "We did not receive anything for her."

Melanie turned to the officer and asked, "Officer, is it not a federal crime to tamper with the U.S. mail?"

"Yes ma'am, it is."

Larger beads of sweat were now pouring down Mr. Jacobson's face. There was a long pause. "Yes, we did," he said finally, exasperated. His wife grabbed his arm and they looked at each other, and communicated with their eyes what needed to be done.

Mrs. Jacobson turned and left the doorway. The group outside waited in silence, and Mr. Jacobson avoided eye contact with anyone, his face now distorted by shame and guilt. His wife returned moments later with a brown manila envelope addressed to Marie Du Bois. She handed it to Melanie, who looked inside the already opened envelope and removed it contents: Marie's passport, stamped on the second page with the permanent resident status seal, and her green card.

Melanie looked up and addressed Mr. Jacobson again. "Sir, were you withholding Ms. Du Bois' documents to use as leverage so that she would give up her baby?" Mr. Jacobson did not respond. "Have you paid Ms. Du Bois her wages for this week?"

He shook his head, "No."

"Well," she continued, "She just delivered a baby and is entitled to some time off from work." Melanie turned to Marie and asked, "Ms. Du Bois, how long have you been working for the Jacobsons?"

Marie finally picked her head up and responded timidly, "almost three years." Melanie turned her attention back to Mr. Jacobson, who now looked furious.

"I think that three weeks paid leave is reasonable, in addition to this week's wage."

There was a moment of complete silence as he stared at Melanie, and she stared back at him, waiting for a response. Then, he walked away from the doorway, followed by his wife. Serena looked at Marie, held her hand and smiled. The police officer leaned against the rail with his arms folded; he also smiled and shook his head. The Jacobsons could be heard arguing quietly inside the home. Moments later, Mr. Jacobson returned and handed Melanie a check. She looked down at it, shook her head in approval, and then gave the envelope and the check to Marie. Mrs. Jacobson returned to the door and handed Melanie a bag with Marie's few belongings.

As they all turned to leave, Melanie said to Mr. Jacobson. "One more thing, Ms. Du Bois will be well within her legal rights to pursue the issue of child support." Mr. Jacobson glared at her and angrily slammed the door shut. Marie was weeping tears of joy as she embraced Melanie, then Karen, then Serena in front of the Jacobson's home. She smiled as Serena had never seen her smile before.

Marie remained at the Hanson's home until the end of the week, and on Friday afternoon she said a tearful goodbye to Karen and the kids as she and her baby, with Serena carrying the bags, boarded the train to begin her life away from circumstances that had brought her both joy and pain.

Chapter 7

It was the middle of August, and almost three months since Serena had been instrumental in helping Marie keep her baby. Rain had drenched most of the central part of the State all week, and the gloom outside was permeating the Hanson's household. There was a quiet tension between Jeff and Karen for about a week, and Serena sensed an emotional storm brewing. It was the night before Serena left for the weekend. She lay awake in her bedroom down the hall from theirs, staring at the ceiling and listening as the quiet argument escalated into shouting.

During the past week, Karen had seemed distracted, tense, upset; she was less patient with the kids and isolated herself in her bedroom. The shouting became louder and Serena could hear every word. "You have been lying to me all along, Jeff," Karen yelled. "I believed you every time you told me you were on call, or working late. All those times you were with her, weren't you?" She was crying. "How long have you been involved with this woman, Jeff?"

"How long, what difference does it make?" Jeff yelled back. "I'm in love with her, there, I've said it, and now you know."

"Why Jeff, what about me and our children, have you forgotten the sacrifices I've made so that you could get through medical school?"

Serena heard the sound of drawers opening and closing; Jeff was obviously packing his clothes. She heard Karen pleading, "Jeff, please don't do this to our family! What about the children?"

"I love my children; that hasn't changed. It's you; I'm not in love with you anymore." There was a moment of silence and as he walked out of the bedroom, he said, "I'll be back for the rest of my things." Serena heard his footsteps leave the bedroom, then stomp down the stairs. Moments later, she heard his Mercedes backing out of the driveway. She got out of bed and looked out the window at the darkness outside; it was still raining. She remembered another time when she was looking out the window staring at the rain. Serena put on her robe and walked down the hallway, gently opening the door of the children's bedroom. Hallie was sitting up in her bed clutching her raggedy ann doll. The dim light of the night table lamp cast a shadow on Connor's face; he was asleep in the twin bed against the opposite wall. Serena walked into the room and sat on Hallie's bed.

"Mommy and daddy are mad at each other," she whispered sadly as Serena put her arms around her and kissed her on the forehead.

"Yes, grownups get mad at each other sometimes, but you young lady should be asleep; tomorrow you have a field trip, remember?" Hallie's face lit up as she slid under her comforter and put her head on the pillow.

Serena closed the door gently behind her and paused for a while, then headed down the hall to Karen's bedroom. She knocked and pushed open the door, Karen was sitting in the middle of their queen size bed, hugging her knees and sobbing quietly. When Serena approached the bed, Karen looked up and said, "He left. I can't believe this is happening. What I am going to tell the children?" Serena sat at the edge of the bed facing Karen. She wanted to say, "When he realizes what he has given up, he'll come back." But she couldn't give her that assurance. She looked at Karen and remembered that not too long ago she herself was crying from the pain of rejection. "Can I get you some chamomile tea?"

Karen shook her head, "Yes."

As she made the tea, Serena remembered the intensity of the emotions she felt the day she discovered that she had lost Nick to another woman; she could identify with the pain Karen was feeling. In her own experience with rejection, there was a recurring, wrenching pain in her chest that paralyzed her whole body and left her emotionally fatigued. When she returned to the bedroom, Karen was on the phone, speaking softly between sobs, a box of tissues in her lap. She looked up. "Thanks." As Serena placed the tea on the night table, she heard Karen say, "Mom, I only recently found out about Jeff and this woman; she is a medical student doing her residency at the hospital." Serena closed the bedroom door quietly, and walked back to her bedroom.

The sound of the doorbell woke Serena, who felt as if she had just fallen asleep. She looked at the clock; it was 3:30 in the morning. The doorbell rang again, but she didn't move. It was probably Jeff. He had changed his mind and come back home, but had forgotten his key when he stormed out earlier she reasoned. She heard Karen going down the stairs, and shortly after she heard her screaming, "No! No! No!" She heard other voices and none of them was Jeff's. Serena ran down the stairs, and was horrified to see a police officer carrying Karen toward the sofa. "She fainted," the officer said, as he laid her gently on the sofa.

As the police officers explained the news he had delivered to Karen, a wave of panic and nausea swept over Serena. Her knees began to feel weak, so she made her way over to the loveseat and slumped into it. While one officer tried to revive Karen, the other went out to the car. He returned with a first aid kit, but while he was opening it, Karen opened her eyes and tried to sit up. "Can you get her a glass of water, please?" one officer asked Serena. When she returned, he had a note pad in his hand and began to ask a series of questions. "Does Mrs. Hanson have relatives in the area? Who is her closest friend?" They needed to contact family members or close friends on her behalf before they left the home. Serena had difficulty focusing to answer their questions, but they were patient, and eventually she was able to locate a phone number for Karen's best friend, Melanie Richardson.

Less than an hour later Melanie arrived, and the officers left. She helped Karen back to the bed and started making phone calls. Serena went into the children's bedroom, and sat in the rocking chair, hugging her knees, gently rocking, and watching them sleep. Grief paralyzed her. Only a few hours ago, Jeff was a handsome, vibrant young man, and now he was gone, dead. According to the police, he must have loss control of his car as it hydroplaned on the wet and slippery westbound side of Highway 78. They determined that he must have been speeding. His Mercedes had hit the median and flipped over, landing on the eastbound side of the highway and was hit by a truck. He was pronounced dead at the scene.

As Serena tried to form a picture in her mind of what happened, she was overwhelmed with sadness. What were Jeff's last thoughts as his car went out of control and he faced the reality of his death? Did he think about the family he had just left or the woman with whom he was planning to start a new life? His last words to his wife were hurtful ones, and his last act was one that would for a long time cause pain for Karen who loved him. She was facing a tragedy that would take her through some dark times emotionally; Serena prayed that God would give her the strength for the tough days ahead.

By late evening, Karen's parents had arrived from Florida. Inconsolable, she was still not able to leave the bedroom. When the kids had awakened that morning, Melanie took them into Karen's bedroom and told them what happened to their father. For a long while the children remained in the bed with their mother, Hallie cried with her and Connor sat clutching his blanket looking at his mother and sister, with an impassive look on his face. Serena focused on taking care of the children's needs, as family members took care of Karen.

The next day, family and friends from everywhere descended upon the home. Jeff's parents, grief stricken at the loss of their only son, made the arrangements for his funeral. The night before the funeral, in a private moment, Karen told Serena that she had decided not to tell Jeff's parents about what happened between them the night he died. "I don't want to burden them with that as well, promise me that you wouldn't say anything?" Serena promised.

During the days immediately following Jeff's funeral, lots of relatives and friends visited the home. They brought cooked meals and baked goods, more than the small family could consume. More importantly, Karen was getting the emotional support she needed. As time passed, however, people returned to their lives, and the constant flow of friends visiting stopped. Karen was on leave from her job, and struggled to just get through the day. She lost the desire to do things, and spent most of the day in her bedroom. Melanie took care of the legal matters related to the accident and Jeff's life insurance. Karen's mother called several times a day. She suggested grief counseling immediately when she realized that Karen was heading into a dark pit of depression.

Serena focused on the housework and caring for the children, keeping things semi-normal for them. She did not go to Brooklyn on the weekends but remained with the family to take the kids out to the movie, the park and other entertainment. Karen's mother returned from Florida three weeks after the funeral when she realized that her daughter was not seeking help through grief counseling. A few days into her mother's visit, Karen called Serena into her bedroom and informed her that she was going to Florida to be with her parents; to get counseling and to have help with the children until she was ready to face life on her own.

Sitting on the edge of the bed together, Karen reached and put her arms around Serena, who was wiping tears from her eyes. It was now the end of a relationship that they both enjoyed. "I am so sorry, but I won't be able to continue with the sponsorship." Karen squeezed her hand. Although this was very disappointing for Serena, it paled in comparison to Karen's loss. Serena looked at her through tear-filled eyes. "Your loss is so much greater than mine. You and Jeff made me feel like a member of your family; I will always remember your kindness. The children will always have a special place in my heart."

Serena helped Karen and the kids pack for their extended trip to Sarasota, Florida, while Karen's mother dutifully got rid of foods in the refrigerator, covered the furniture and went around the home unplugging electrical appliances. Melanie promised to forward the mail and take care of the house while they were away. The taxi took Serena to the train station first before taking the shattered Hanson family to Newark airport. As they stood on the curb, Karen embraced Serena and whispered, "Thanks so much for being there for me and the kids. I don't think I could have made it without your kindness and patience." The kids came out of the car to say goodbye. Serena hugged Hallie, who said sadly, "I love you." Connor, who was excited about going on the airplane, hugged Serena's legs and said, "Bye, see you later alligator." It was difficult leaving the sidewalk; Serena did not want this part of her life to end. She watched the taxi until it was out of sight, and then took one last look at the quaint downtown area of Summit, with its boutiques and shops, that had become so familiar to her. Then, picking up the duffle bag with her belongings, she slowly walked to the train station to face new uncertainties.

Chapter 8

After many years in disagreement dispute with Guatemala and British involvement to prevent threatened invasion by Guatemala, Belize gained its independence on September 21, 1981. Celebration parties were planned that weekend in all five boroughs of New York City in the communities where Belizeans lived.

Emma planned to attend a fund raising party on Saturday night at a trendy nightclub in Brooklyn, hoping to reconnect with old friends from Belize. It was also her chance to get Serena out of the apartment, where for the past week she had been sequestered in a melancholy mood. She was troubled by the tragedy of Jeff's sudden death and Karen's overwhelming grief. She was stunned by how quickly circumstances could change the course of people's lives. She was also disillusioned about losing sponsorship from such a good family. The memory of the woman crying at the Jonah Employment agency haunted her, and she feared the uncertainty of the sponsorship process.

Emma had a difficult time convincing Serena that she was going to have fun at the Club that night. She opened the doors to her closet. "Choose any dress and it's yours," Emma coaxed her. Serena moved the hangers along the rod slowly and without enthusiasm.

"Maybe this one," she declared, removing a hanger with a black dress. It was fitted at the waistline with thin shoulder straps, the full chiffon skirt reaching just below the knees as she held it against her body.

"Good choice," Emma exclaimed happily. "I'll get matching accessories." She reached below the dresses, into some boxes and presented the shoes. Then, she danced to the other side of the room to a smaller closest and announced, "Ta dah, this is perfect," handing Serena a small purse made of silver beads.

"I'll be wearing this, purchased for the occasion," Emma exclaimed joyfully, removing the Macy's plastic garment bag to reveal a beautiful, red halter dress with a full skirt also reaching just below the knees.

Later that evening, dressed fashionably, Emma and Serena got out of the taxi cab in front of the CALYPSO Club where a small crowd were standing around the entrance. The men were shaking hands, slapping each other on the shoulders, and the women, stylishly dressed, stood together talking and laughing. Emma and Serena did not recognize anyone as they made their way to the entrance; they presented their tickets to the man standing inside the door and went in.

Inside the club, the music was loud; Serena could feel the vibration in her chest. She hated that feeling; it made her anxious as if a panic attack was coming on. A few people were on the dance floor, but most sat around large round tables that lined the walls. The lights were dim; it was difficult at first to distinguish faces as they made their way to a vacant table. A waitress came over as soon as they sat down and asked if they wanted something from the bar. She bent closer and Emma ordered a virgin pina colada. Serena shouted, "I'll have the same." Shortly after the waitress returned with their drinks, the people who had been standing outside came in and began occupying the rest of the tables.

The music stopped suddenly, the lights were turned up, the people who were dancing took their seats and the DJ walked to the center of the room.

"Thank you, my fellow Belizeans, for coming out to celebrate this momentous occasion for our country. Belize is now an independent nation, we have the freedom to shape our own destiny. Let us pray for and support our leaders in government, and ask God to bless our country." He paused as if praying silently. "Tonight's celebration party is also a fund-raiser for a new Independence Day scholarship fund. It will be used to support students from Belize to travel abroad to study." He unwrapped something he was holding in his hand. It was the new Belizean flag; a loud cheer rose from the crowd. The DJ waved the flag then took his place behind the musical equipment. He played continuous soca and calypso hits from Belize and the Caribbean.

Feeling a soft tap on her shoulder, Emma turned around, and let out an ecstatic cry; she jumped to her feet and into the arms of a tall, lean, good looking young man dressed in a tan suit. He had the biggest smile and whitest teeth Serena had ever seen. Emma was shouting above the music, "Pete, what a surprise, I didn't know you were in New York, last I heard you were in Canada!" She was holding his hands until they sat down. She shouted across the table, "Serena, this is Pete. We grew up in the same neighborhood back home, went to the same church, the same school." Pete reached across the table and shook Serena's hand. Then, as if no one else was in the room, Emma and Pete talked and laughed, leaning closer to hear each other above the loud music. Before long, they were on the dance floor. The lights were turned down again and bodies were swaying in every direction to the rhythm of the beat. Serena was not feeling the exuberance of the celebration. She sat as an observer, and declined gracefully when she was invited to dance.

"What's the matter with your friend?" Pete asked Emma during a slow dance together.

Emma looked over in Serena's direction and said to Pete, "Let's talk in the hallway." Pete followed her to the hallway near the bathrooms, where she quietly explained Serena's predicament.

Pete thought for a moment, then said, "I heard about a lawyer who has some connections and have been getting green cards for people in a few months."

"Really, is it legit?" Emma asked suspiciously.

"Well, a friend at work told me he got his through this lawyer; I could get the details from him for you."

They returned to the table and Emma whispered to Serena what Pete had told her. Serena looked skeptically at both of them.

"It's worth a try," declared Emma, ever the optimist.

Pete had to leave the party early; so he took Emma's contact information and promised to stop by her apartment the next evening to give them more details. Besides Pete, Emma and Serena did not recognize anyone at the party, which was disappointing, so after Pete left they no longer had the desire to stay. They were walking to the exit, when Emma suddenly pulled Serena onto the dance floor, and shouted, "Come on, you have to dance at least one song before we leave." Serena laughed, and started to dance, feeling awkward as she moved her arms, hips and feet to the rhythm of the music, trying to please Emma, though she was not truly enjoying the moment. It was 2:00 a.m. when they were finally in a taxi cab on their way home and Serena suddenly felt a spark of hope, ignited by Pete's promise.

🎕 🎕

Two days after the party at the club, Pete visited Emma and Serena at the apartment as he had promised. He explained all that he knew about the lawyer who guaranteed speedy processing of the green card for a fee. However, when Serena heard the details, she became suspicious and was reluctant to commit to something she told Emma was, "Too good to be true." Pete insisted that it went well for his co-worker, and did not see any reason why the outcome wouldn't be the same for her. Emma reminded Serena of her only option: another live-in housekeeping or nanny position, with no guarantees of successful sponsorship. Soon, Serena was talking herself into the idea. If it meant seeing her son sooner rather than later, she reasoned, it would be worth every penny. A couple days passed before Pete called to say that he contacted the lawyer on her behalf, and a date and time was set for their first meeting.

The meeting place was at the precinct on the corner of Varick and Moore streets, near busy China Town in lower Manhattan. Pete circled the block several times before finding a parking space. As they walked toward the precinct, Serena wrestled with conflicting thoughts, but remained quiet about it. They were almost at the main entrance when a black Cadillac pulled up to the curb. A man with thick graying hair and a well-tanned complexion got out of the passenger side of the car and began walking toward them. He appeared professional, dressed in a gray stripped suit and carrying a black attaché case. As he closed the distance between them, he smiled and stretched out his hand. He shook Pete's hand first, then said, "And you, young lady, must be Serena Miller." His grip was firm as he shook her hand. "I'm Frank Papalado; let's go inside." He led the way to the double doors, after turning to gesture with his hand to the man behind the wheel of the Cadillac.

The precinct was noisy as police officers boisterously communicated with each other, and the voices over the police radios blared from all directions. For a moment they stood just inside the entrance. Serena's eyes were adjusting to the lighting and her ears to the auditory overload when something brushed against her leg startling her. It was a German shepherd heading for the door with a police officer in tow. Sensing her hesitation to move forward, Frank held her by the arm and led her to the counter; Pete sat on a bench and waited. A police officer appeared from behind a side door and shook hands with Frank; they appeared to know each other very well.

"Lou, this young lady needs to be finger printed." The police officer opened the side door and ushered them in. He took control of her hands at the finger printing station, moving each finger on the pad as if they weren't attached to her, and speaking with Frank about the Yankees game on television the night before. The men continued to chat as she went to the sink in the far corner to wash her hands. When she returned, Frank asked for her passport, which he handed to the police officer who copied information onto the finger print card. He then handed both to Frank. "Thanks Lou, see you Saturday."

"Yeah," Lou responded, and proceeded to clean the finger printing area.

Just outside the main entrance door, Frank said in a low voice, "I will contact you as soon as we need to schedule your interview with INS." He reached into his jacket pocket and took out a small writing pad. "Give me your current address and phone number." He wrote down the information, then added, "I need to keep your passport. Of course, you'll get it back at the end." Serena handed Frank an envelope with $800, the first of two payments for his service. He put the envelope, her passport and finger-printed card in his attaché case, said goodbye to them, and walked to the Cadillac, still parked at the curb waiting for him. Serena got a strange feeling in the pit of her stomach. She fought the impulse to run after him and say, "Sorry, I've changed my mind." But that would be embarrassing, especially for Pete. So she stood for awhile and stared at him as he got into the car, leaving with her passport and money.

She was quiet on the ride back to Brooklyn. Pete sensed that she was anxious and tried to reassure her, "Things will work out just fine; in a few months you'll be smiling when you get your green card." When she did not respond, he continued, "Sometimes, the reward is worth the risk." Serena finally forced a smile. "You're right; I should be hoping for the best, not worrying." However, she had a difficult time falling asleep that night; so far all of her risks had not yielded rewards, and she was uneasy about the path she just took.

❧❦ ❦❧

A week after her meeting with Frank, Serena became more hopeful, mainly because of encouraging words from Pete and Emma. "Hope for the best," they said. "Don't think the worse." So she made peace with her decision. However, she was reminded of Aunt Julia's words about forcing doors open that are closed for a reason.

Taking the advice of an acquaintance at the church she and Emma attended, Serena went to a different employment agency to find work. This time, she accepted a live-out child care position in lower Manhattan, working for a single mother with two young children. Her new employer was a hair stylist in an upscale beauty salon in mid Manhattan. She was a petite figured, pretty woman with olive tone skin, thick curly brown hair, who dressed very stylishly. She was from South Africa and had moved to the United States six years ago. The recently divorced mother lived with her two young children on the third floor of a four-story walk-up building with a deli store on the main floor. Miriam said she was looking for a trustworthy person to take care of the children; prepare their meals, entertain them, and keep them safe.

Serena fell in love with the children as soon as she laid eyes on them. Myckala was 5 years old with milk white skin, black, shining, wavy hair that she constantly tried to keep out of her face and green eyes with longer than normal eye lashes. Rowie was almost three, with cheeks like cherub angels and deep dimples that appeared when he smiled. Unlike his sister he had straight, thick dark brown hair that framed his adorable face. Each morning after their mom left for work, Serena made the children breakfast and then walked Myckala to school four blocks away, pushing Rowie in a stroller. She liked being out and about in the hustle and bustle of the city. When she picked up Myckala from school in the afternoon, if the weather was nice, she packed a snack and took them to the park to play. There, she met other mothers and nannies who also routinely took their children to play. The children and Serena began to develop friendships at the park.

There was not much work to do in the one bedroom apartment. The living room was large with dark hardwood flooring and high ceiling. The small kitchen included a washer and dryer near the sink, and the door to the tiny bathroom were near the entrance into the kitchen. The one bedroom was small, and had two twin beds for the children which took up much of the space in the room. The mother slept in an elevated loft type bed, built of wood against one of the walls in the open living room; it had four support beams and a ladder. Under the loft and between the four support beams was a dining table with four chairs.

The only three windows in the apartment faced the front of the building and overlooked the busy street. Miriam had lined the outside space between the window sills and the iron guard rails of the fire escape, with potted plants that Serena enjoyed watering and pruning. The children had been taught by their mother to clean up after themselves and to put their toys away in boxes and baskets. She was a very neat woman, so she left little housework for Serena to do, besides making the kids beds and doing their laundry every couple days.

Serena enjoyed taking care of the children, who were happy and affectionate. She was forming a special attachment to Rowie, who reminded her of her son Benjamin. Sometimes, he sat on her lap and they cuddled while they watched Sesame Street in the mornings after Myckala went to school. Mostly, Serena sat on the floor and played with him; coloring, doing puzzles, reading him stories, and teaching him the alphabet.

She saw the children's father every other Friday when he came to the apartment to take them for the weekend. He spoke English with a heavy accent, smiled easily, was very polite and appeared to be shy. He always seemed overwhelmed by emotions when he saw his children, who were happy and eager to go with him. He said very little to Serena, but every time she handed him the children's overnight bag, he handed her $20 and whispered "Thank you." On those Fridays, Serena left work earlier than usual. Miriam always paid her in the morning before she left for work, so she locked the apartment and left soon after the children left with their father.

❧ ❧

Serena enjoyed the freedom of going home each day to the apartment she shared with Emma, and in the six months she had been working for Miriam she felt good about things. Letters from her friend Valerie kept her abreast of the latest happenings in San Ignacio and more importantly how Benny was doing. On two occasions, Valerie had sent pictures of him, which Serena was tempted to leave in Nick's mailbox, but she didn't.

Four months after their first meeting, Frank Papalado, contacted Serena by phone, assured her that her petition was in the final stage of approval, and she would soon be notified by mail about her appointment date. She was ecstatic. The day after the phone call she met him near the subway on her way to work and gave him the remaining $800.00 of his $1,600.00 fee.

Chapter 9

It was Friday morning, and Emma felt she needed a mental health day and a three-day weekend. It had been several months since she had taken a day off, so she called her supervisor at the bank to let her know that she was taking a personal day. Shortly after Serena left for work Emma climbed back into bed, tucked the comforter around her, hugged her pillow, took a deep breath, and closed her eyes hoping to invite sleep back into her day. But sleep did not come immediately as she hoped; her thoughts crossed the ocean and landed in Belize.

Emma missed her family, friends, home and neighborhood, but she was beginning to like the life she was creating in America. Her mother used to say that she had an "independent spirit." Childhood memories like an old movie started playing in her mind. She was blessed with loving parents who worked hard to give all four children the best they could afford. They had stressed the importance of education, good work ethics, and had taught them to be confident in their abilities. Emma's excellent grades earned her an all expense paid scholarship to attend a university in the United States. Her two older brothers had continued their higher education in Canada and England, and had both chosen to remain in those countries. Her younger sister was in her senior year of high school in Belize.

Emma was 18 years when she left home to attend Pace University. The move from a small town to New York City required adjustments that were sometimes difficult. She cried in her dorm room many times when she was overwhelmed by the hectic pace of six classes and working 15 hours a week in the Registrar's Office. Emma smiled, as she remembered all the things that had made her shed tears. But now she was content. She loved her job, her cozy apartment, and her small circle of friends. She was especially happy to have Serena living with her; they got along really well. She was also happy now that she had reconnected with Pete, who was becoming a good friend to both of them. It was somewhere in that state of contentment that Emma drifted off to sleep.

The clock on the night table next to her bed showed 12:42 p.m. when Emma awoke for the second time that day. She was hungry, so after making a trip to the bathroom, she headed to the kitchen. A few minutes later, she was sitting on the sofa with a tuna sandwich on a plate in her lap, a tall glass of pink lemonade on the coffee table and the remote control in her hand. The TV came on with the introduction to *All My Children*. Emma sat through all the afternoon soaps with intense interest. She realized now why some viewers became hooked on soap operas; such passion, such drama, such extreme emotions, she was riveted to the TV screen. During a commercial break, Emma hurried to take a bathroom break, she got a can of mixed nuts from the kitchen, headed back to the sofa and did not move again until *General Hospital* ended, with Luke and Laura locked in a kiss in a dim and empty night club. "Wow," Emma said out loud as she turned off the TV and took her dishes to the kitchen. Maybe it was time to buy a VCR, she thought, to tape the soaps during the day while she was at work, and watch them at night ……maybe.

Emma took a shower and got dressed. She decided that when Serena got home from work, they would go out to eat; she felt like having something ethnic and spicy. Serena usually got home between 5:30 and 6:00 p.m., so Emma was dressed and ready at 5:15. She found the latest *Ebony* magazine she had not yet read, sat on the sofa, and turned on the TV to watch the evening news. The image that appeared on the screen got her attention. Two police officers were escorting a tall, middle-aged man dressed in a gray suit out of a building and leading him to a police car. Behind them was another man also surrounded by police officers being lead to another police car. Reporters with microphones in their hands were running towards the first man as the officers pushed him into the car. The screen switched back to the newsroom and the anchor woman said, "Frank Papalado along with his driver were two of the six people arrested today in Brooklyn for taking money from illegal immigrants and fraudulently obtaining green cards for them." Emma sat upright; she felt a chill rush through her body. The news anchor continued, "The FBI was informed of the illegal activities by an informant, and will be investigating the INS office to see if someone on the inside was part of this ring." The camera turned on the male anchor, "In other news......." Emma turned the television off. She needed to process what she had just seen and heard to prepare the right words to say to Serena.

"I don't believe this," Serena said before she collapsed onto the sofa, burying her face in one of the pillows. Emma sat next to her and gently rubbed her back, comforting her, but in that instance it was as if a dark cloud was hovering over the apartment, and it remained there all weekend as Serena either remained in her room or walked around the apartment looking defeated.

The loud knocking on the door startled them both as they were gathering their things to leave for work on Monday morning. Neither of them moved to open it, fearing who may be on the other side. The knock was louder and longer the second time. Emma took her shoes off, tip toed to the door and looked through the peep hole. As she pulled away and turned to Serena with a look of horror on her face, she whispered, "Two men in uniform." Serena gasped, covered her mouth with both hands, and immediately the muscles in her stomach tightened into a knot. "Let's pretend we are not home," Emma whispered as she paced quietly back and forth.

The knocking was now replaced by the sound of a fist pounding on the door. She sighed, walked toward the door and unlocked the two deadbolt locks, leaving the security chain attached.

"Yes, can I help you?" She calmly asked.

As if the movement was rehearsed, both men instantly whipped out their ID badges and held them up to her gaze. The taller, bigger man with a well-groomed mustache said, "Morning, ma'am; we are INS officers." He paused, waiting to see her reaction. "Are you Serena Miller?"

"No sir." Emma shook her head, hoping her answer was enough to make them leave.

The other man stepped closer and asked, "Does she live at this address?"

Emma paused; she was tempted to say "no," but fearing she might make the situation worse by lying, finally answered, "Yes, she lives here."

"I'm Officer McCain and this is Officer O'Brian; we would like to ask her some questions."

Emma removed the chain and opened the door. Once inside, the men appeared to be less intimidating, but their presence seemed to fill the room. The larger of the two reached into his jacket pocket and produced a passport. He looked at the picture, then at Serena, who was standing against the wall in the hallway, paralyzed by fear. "Ma'am, does this passport belong to you?" He held it open and showed it to her. She shook her head "yes," avoiding his eyes. He continued, "We found this in the possession of Frank Papalado when he was arrested recently on charges of fraud. He was part of a ring securing residency status for illegal aliens for money." He paused before continuing. "Ma'am, did you enter into the country illegally?" Serena kept her head down and did not respond. He asked, "Are you working without a work permit?"

After a long pause, she finally shook her head. "Yes," she uttered, still not looking at him.

"It is a federal offense to enter the country illegally and to work without a permit; we have to take you into custody."

Serena stood motionless, and could feel her heart pounding against the wall of her chest, as she processed what he said. She heard Emma gasp, "Oh no!"

"She will be in custody until she goes before an INS judge." The man continued with his attention now on Emma. Serena, still glued to the wall, heard them give the location of the detention center and the phone number to Emma. "Call the number for information on visiting hours and what she is allowed to have while in detention."

Emma walked toward her friend, peeled her away from the wall and hugged her. The two held each other for awhile, but said nothing. Soon, Serena was walking between the two uniformed men to the large black car parked across the street from the entrance of the apartment building.

Initially, there was silence in the car as they drove through the streets of Brooklyn just before the morning rush hour. They were stopped at an intersection by a school crossing guard. Seeing the children crossing the street, Serena suddenly remembered Mycala and Rowie, and that she was getting ready to leave for work before her life was interrupted. She began to feel sick in her stomach as she thought of Miriam waiting for her to arrive to leave for work. "They will think horribly of me," she thought as her eyes began to burn with the tears filling them. While she was preoccupied with those thoughts, the men had begun to talk about football teams, their favorite players and the game they had watched the night before. They were boisterous; it was as if she wasn't in the back seat of the car. She wished she wasn't and that this was a nightmare from which she would gradually awake. But minutes later, she was escorted into the main entrance of a detention center. The men handed her and her passport over to two ladies wearing the same uniform, and sitting behind a counter in the receiving area.

The short, stocky woman with short, bleach blonde hair, pointed to a bench in the hallway and told her to sit and wait to be processed. After what seemed like an eternity, sitting, waiting, she was ushered into an office by the other female officer who had the deep, raspy voice of a smoker. Serena sat across from her at a desk with nothing on it except a neat pile of folders on one side. The woman took a folder and some forms from shelves behind her, and for the next hour she asked questions, often without looking up, and wrote down the answers without comment or any friendly gesture.

By 11:30 a.m. the questioning was finally over, and again she was asked to sit on the bench and wait. This time the hallway was not as isolated; people were walking back and forth past her and she could hear the sounds of male voices behind the wall where she was sitting. At noon, the woman who had interviewed her brought her a tray with a ham and cheese sandwich, an apple and a can of grape soda. "When you are finished eating, I'll take you inside," she said before leaving. Serena was hungry and it didn't take her long to eat the sandwich and drink the soda. She was staring at the deep, rich, red color of the apple in her hand when the woman came back and said, "Come with me please." She left the tray on the seat and followed her into a changing room. "While you are here, you have to wear these." She handed Serena an orange one piece suit and a plastic bag with toiletries, socks and undergarments. She was allowed to keep her socks and sneakers on, but was instructed to fold her clothing and put them into a brown paper bag that already had her name printed on it in large black letters.

After she had changed into the orange suit, she was led into a lounge with sofas, chairs and a television mounted on the wall; it was on but no one was watching it. Five women wearing the same orange one piece suit were in the room; they all sat apart from each other. One was sitting in the far corner with her arms folded across her chest, her head bent downward and her eyes closed. Three were turning the pages of magazines they had retrieved from the pile on the table in the center of the room. The fifth woman was reading a book, occasionally lifting her head and staring at the ceiling as if trying to remember something.

Serena settled into a corner of the big sofa in the middle of the room and turned her attention to the television. *All My Children* was on. She had started watching that soap opera while Rowie took his nap and before it was time to pick Myckala up from school. Now, she wondered again what Miriam had done about work and the children; she felt awful about upsetting their routine. She tried to focus on the soaps to provide a distraction from the worrying.

The hours seemed to drag between lunch and dinner. The lounge was full of gloom. No one spoke. They just sat and waited. Later, they were ushered into in a small dining area to eat dinner. Some of the women hardly touched their meal. After dinner, they were escorted back to the lounge, where some of the women went back to their solitude, while others, including Serena, stared at the television, watching the nightly sitcoms that provided a welcome break from the reality of their present circumstances.

At 8 p.m., the two night shift female officers came in and announced that it was time for lockdown. They were allowed to use the bathroom, two at a time. When they had all finished their hygiene break, they were led down a hallway to the cells. The guards called out their names and cell numbers. Once they were inside by pairs, the iron doors were locked. Serena's cell mate was the tall woman with ebony skin and long braided hair, who had sat by herself in the corner all day, had not touched her food, and appeared to be in a state of shock. She sat on the edge of the bed with her head cupped in her hands, staring at the floor. "Lights out in 10 minutes, ladies," one of the guards called out. Serena settled into the bed, laid on her back, pulled the blanket to her chin, and stared at the ceiling. She wanted to wallow in her own pity, but was preoccupied with the woman sitting on the bed across from her. She wanted to say something, but could not think of the right words to say. "Are you okay?" seemed a ridiculous question, so she remained quiet and stared at the white ceiling with the single dull light barely illuminating the room. The woman began to cry quietly when the lights went out and she continued to sit for about an hour, before finally settling into the bed.

Sleep did not come easily that night. Serena's mind was too busy trying to adjust to life back in Belize. She had spent almost two years planning to embrace the opportunities in America: education, career, a family, a home, "The American Dream." She had imagined Benny attending school here and growing up in this diverse culture. But now she worried about the basics of life, finding work in Belize, being able to support the two of them, and living on her own.

After everyone had taken their shower and eaten breakfast, the second day at the detention center passed pretty much like the first, except that after dinner Serena received a call from Emma, who promised to visit the next day. Also, her cell mate had a visitor: a young, well-groomed black man wearing a navy blue suit and carrying a brief case. After his visit, the woman seemed less distraught, but she was still avoiding conversation, even in the cell room.

On Wednesday morning after breakfast, Serena was called into an office and interviewed by someone from the court who informed her that she was scheduled to see the INS judge on Friday at 11 a.m. The court officer described the proceedings and explained the reasons why there was a high probability for immediate deportation. Later that afternoon, she was happy to see her friend Emma, who brought a small travel bag, packed with some of her clothing, a pair of shoes, toiletries, makeup, and her purse with the money from her last week's pay. She was relieved to learn that Emma had called her employer to explain her sudden absence that morning. Emma was teary eyed, sad about losing a good friend and roommate. Pete, she said, was also very upset about the way things turned out, and blamed himself for her predicament.

Shortly after Emma left, the women were called to dinner. They seemed friendlier toward each other; some looked relieved of a burden after their meeting with the court official. The conversations Serena overheard all centered on the circumstances that brought them to the detention center. The woman from the Philippines had paid a man $5,000 to marry her, but he never showed up the day they were scheduled to get married at City Hall. Later, in the lounge, Serena sat next to her cell mate, who finally smiled. "I am sorry I have not been friendly," she said quietly. "My name is Naomi." She reached out her right hand; Serena took it and replied, "I'm Serena."

"I was very scared and worried when I first came here, because I can't go back home; they would probably kill me." When she saw the expression on Serena's face change from a smile to disbelief, she began to tell her story. Serena stared at her flawless face and was fascinated by her unusual pronunciation of English words. Naomi was from a poor village in South Africa. At age 15, her father promised her in marriage to a man in a neighboring village who already had four wives and 19 children. She was fearful of the man because of his known cruelty to his wives, who worked as slaves maintaining his livestocks and farming his land. There were rumors in the village that he was involved with beatings and killings in the Apartheid struggle against the South African government.

She had run away to Johannesburg before the marriage with the help of her 20 year-old brother, who also helped secure a job for her as a nanny with an English couple who had two small children. Naomi was very tall at 15 and appeared to be older; she told the couple she was 18. After working with them for about one year, the British Company who employed the husband needed him to return to the home office in England. Naomi begged to go with them; she was fearful of being on her own in Johannesburg, and even more fearful of returning to the village where she would surely be beaten for dishonoring her father, and forced into the marriage. Somehow, the British couple got the necessary documents to take her along with them to England.

At the end of the third year working with them in England, the couple was being transferred to Australia. The children were now 5 and 7 and were in school full time, so the family no longer needed to have a nanny. They could not take her to Australia and suggested she travel to America, where she had a maternal aunt living in

New York with whom she had been corresponding in recent years. They helped her secure a vacation visa and provided the airfare for her travel. She was in the United States for about one year, working as a maid at a hotel in Manhattan, and was using her cousin's social security number to maintain employment.

Naomi's trouble began when she started dating a man who also worked at the hotel as a security guard. He had told her that he was divorced which turned out to be false, and she was confronted by his wife. After the initial embarrassing verbal confrontation in front of the hotel, threatening phone calls from his wife about reporting her followed, and soon thereafter the INS officers were at her door. However, she was hopeful now that she had spoken to the lawyer her aunt had retained. He said that she could challenge the deportation, and request asylum based on persecution if she returned to South Africa. It would cost a lot in legal fees to fight the deportation, but she was willing to spend all she had in savings to do so. As Serena's thoughts formulated the words, *another casualty of the coveted green card*. Naomi asked, "Can't you get a lawyer?" Serena explained that she did not have any options. There was no political, social or religious implications if she returned to Belize; she had entered the US illegally, worked without a work permit, and had tried to secure a green card through fraud. She would be fighting a losing battle to challenge any decision.

Friday morning was just as she envisioned: An old grumpy judge, looking above the rim of his glasses in disgust, his eyes lingering on some longer than on others. He spoke dispassionately to the detainees as he looked over their files. They were seen three at a time in the same hour and one by one their fates were determined. Naomi was the only one in their group with a paid attorney, who pleaded brilliantly for asylum which the judge granted. The other women, like Serena, had court appointed officers, who stood next to them as the judge questioned and reprimanded them on their criminal actions. She was not surprised when the judge stared at her long and hard. His glasses slid to the tip of his nose and his wrinkled face looked angry. "Miss Miller, I rule for immediate deportation back to your country of origin." He picked up a wooden stamp, stamped several times on the papers in front of him, and closed her file.

Serena was alone in her cell that night; Naomi had left with her attorney shortly after her hearing. She sat in the bed, embracing her knees with her arms and resting her head upon them. She reflected on everything, from the night she crossed the river, to sitting in the cell as a criminal. Nick occupied her thoughts, but only as perpetrator of all her troubles.

On Saturday, she was informed by an officer shortly after breakfast that she would be deported on Monday. The four other women were being deported on different days in that same week. They spent the weekend together, encouraging each other and talking about the life they had left behind and would return to. Serena was allowed a phone call, she called Emma, it was a tearful goodbye.

Chapter 10

The day of Serena's deportation came quickly, too quickly. Shortly after breakfast, she was dressed and ready to leave. There was an exchange of documents between the officers on the morning shift and the two officers accompanying her to JFK International Airport.

The airline announced that the flight to Miami was delayed, Serena wondered what would happen if she missed the connecting flight to Belize. She was told earlier that an INS officer would receive her off the airplane in Miami and escort her onto the airplane bound for Belize. The two female officers sat with her near the boarding gate; she was in the middle of them, clutching her purse, her small travel bag next to her feet. Serena felt like a trapped animal. She looked at the people rushing back and forth in the terminal with envy, wondering how many took for granted their freedom to enter and leave without consequences.

"I have to use the restroom," Serena said, interrupting the female officers' conversation. She pushed the travel bag with her feet under the seat, and still clutching her small purse, walked to the women's restroom, accompanied by one of the officers. There was a line of about five women waiting ahead of her; she joined the line with the officer standing next to her, prompting inquiring stares from women as they walked pass. The officer, sensing Serena's uneasiness and embarrassment, whispered, "I'll wait outside." Serena appreciated her thoughtfulness.

A cleaning lady was putting paper towels in the paper holder at the far end of the restroom. When she turned to push her cleaning cart in the direction of the waiting line, Serena saw something familiar: A painted picture on the front of her tee shirt of Belize's coral reefs, and BELIZE printed above it in bold blue letters. As the woman approached, their eyes met. The two women ahead of Serena in the line moved forward to use the available stalls, leaving Serena alone in the line.

"Excuse me Miss, you from Belize?" Serena asked quietly.

The woman smiled and responded, "Yes, I'm from Belmopan, you from Belize too?"

"Yes, I'm from San Ignacio." Serena forced a smile.

"Going home for vacation, eh?" The woman touched her forearm with a curious excitement on her face.

Serena did not respond immediately, she looked around and leaned closer to the woman. She whispered, "I'm being deported, but I don't want to go back this way."

The woman's eyes widened, "What happened?" Her expression changed to deep concern.

Serena looked around again, women were washing and drying their hands; no one was paying attention to them. "It's a long story, but a week ago I was arrested by INS officers at my friend's apartment in Brooklyn. The judge ordered immediate deportation, so today I am being sent back to Belize."

The woman parked her cart against the wall. She waited until Serena came out of the stall, and was washing her hands at the sink. Moving closer to her, she whispered, "Come with me." Serena hesitated. She looked around, noticing they were alone for that brief moment. "Come," the woman insisted. She followed the cleaning lady to the far end of the restroom. Behind them, toilets were flushing, doors were opening, and faucets were running, but Serena did not look back. The woman unlocked a door that opened into a room with shelves of cleaning supplies, lockers lining the walls, and a bench in the middle of the open space.

She closed the door behind them and whispered, "You could get away." She pointed to another door. With those words, Serena felt her body tremble. "That door will let you out of the building at the back of the terminal. Then, go to the front where the taxis are parked waiting for fares and take one back to Brooklyn." The woman moved quickly, opening one of the lockers and pulling out her handbag. She scribbled on a piece of paper and handed it to Serena.

"This is my address and phone number, take the taxi to my place, I will call my daughter to let her know." She opened her wallet, "Here!" She gave Serena a $20 bill, "For the taxi cab."

The woman went back into the locker and pulled out a denim shirt and a white cap. "Here, put this shirt on, and pull your hair back under the cap." Serena responded to the woman's instructions without thinking, and altered her appearance quickly. The woman also quickly changed into a plain blue tee-shirt that she snatched out of her locker, and stuffed the Belize shirt into her bag.

"I'll have to get back out there quickly and start cleaning, in a few minutes they'll be searching for you, go quickly!"

"Thank you," Serena hugged her. "What's your name?"

"Anna," the woman answered, pushing her away, "Now go, and be careful."

🖙 🖚

The glare of the sunlight blinded her when she pushed open the heavy door; Serena squinted until her eyes could focus, then stepped onto the platform at the top of the stairs leading down to the back of the building near the parking lot. She paused, took a deep breath and looked around. The huge parking lot was surrounded by buildings, some with large cargo planes parked in front of them. In the distance, people were milling about, but the area beneath the stairs was isolated. She stepped onto the first step and headed quickly down to the ground. The noise level from engines humming heightened her sense of urgency to escape. However, when she got to the bottom of the stairs, she was not sure whether to go right or left to get to the front of the building. Anna's directions had been vague. To her right, she noticed an open area, and hoped it was the ground level parking lot; she could use the cars as cover as she tried to find her way to the taxi cabs.

Serena began to walk quickly along the side of the building, but the consequences of being caught scared her into running. So focused on reaching the opening, she did not see the gaping hole in the cement pavement. Her momentum was suddenly interrupted, her body jerked forward and dropping her purse; she landed on her outstretched hands. Almost immediately she felt a sharp pain radiating from her left ankle. Quickly lifting herself off the ground, Serena picked up her purse and looked at her bruised palms. She tried to resume running, but couldn't because of the pain in her left foot; so she hopped on her right foot toward the opening in the building.

A parked police car came into view as she neared the entrance of the ground floor parking garage. She panicked, hopping away from the entrance toward the nearest cars in the open parking lot; she crouched down between a red car and a white van. From her crouched position, she looked up and realized that she could easily be seen from the large windows of the terminal building. Serena became desperate to conceal herself from view of the windows overhead and from an approaching vehicle. The door of the car was locked. She jostled the handle on the side door of the white van; it was unlocked. She climbed in quickly, pulled the door shut and squatted between the second and third row seats. She decided to wait for the right moment to try again to get a taxi cab.

The approaching vehicle stopped somewhere near the white van. Slowly, Serena eased up from her crouched position to look. She saw a small vehicle similar to a golf cart with two men. One got off and she saw his profile only briefly, his back was facing her as he continued to speak to the man behind the wheel. After a moment, they shook hands and the man headed toward the white van. Serena crouched down again and made herself into a ball. She whispered frantically, "Please, please, not this van." But the driver's door opened, closed, the engine turned on and the van began to move. Fear gripped her. She took deep breaths to try to calm the panic rising inside of her stomach.

It was difficult maintaining her position between the seats with the vigorous movements of the van, hopping over speed bumps, stopping, starting and turning sharply. She hoped the driver would have a reason to stop soon, so that she could escape and catch a train to Brooklyn, to Anna's house. Twenty minutes passed. The van was driving at highway speed. Her left ankle was throbbing with pain. Serena slowly and carefully moved herself into a long sitting position, straightening her legs from under her.

The driver whistled on and off to songs on the radio and occasionally tapped on the steering wheel like it was his drum. About 45 minutes had gone by and Serena began to feel pain in her lower back as her body in this tense position felt the impact of every bump on the road. She wondered if making her presence known would scare or anger the man. She desperately needed to get up from the floor into a more comfortable position, the pain in her ankle now throbbing relentlessly.

The sneeze was sudden; it came out before she could muffle the sound. The van jerked as the driver suddenly slammed the brake. "Hey, who's back there?" he yelled. She felt the van turn sharply to the right and slowed to a stop.

The driver's door opened, followed by the passenger door. Serena hastily covered her face with her hands. "What on earth are you doing in here?" the man asked sternly.

Slowly, she lowered her hands, but did not look at his face. "I was hiding," she said just above a whisper.

"Why in this van?" The man's voice was more surprised than angry, but she was still afraid to look at him.

With her eyes still lowered, she replied, "I was trying to get away from some people at the airport, but I fell and I hurt my ankle before I could get to a taxi." He seemed to be waiting for more explanation. She continued. "I climbed into your van to hide, but you drove away before I could get out." Gradually, she raised her head and eyes to look at him.

"I can't believe you've been in this uncomfortable position in a moving van for almost an hour." He looked concern, and then added, "Well, there's no need to hide anymore; sit on the seat."

Serena had difficulty getting to her feet because of the pain in her left ankle, so the man offered his hand and helped her get up and into the second row seat. Cars and trucks were speeding past; he had pulled off to the side of a major highway.

"Is this the Bronx?" Serena asked, looking around.

"No, we're between Yonkers and Connecticut, about 30 minutes from where I am headed, to Danbury." He settled back into the driver's seat, took off his sun glasses and turned to look at her. For a moment, they stared at each other. She looked at his brown, straight tussled hair, the chiseled angular features of his face and steel gray eyes under hooded brows.

He broke the silence. "Now these people you are running from, who are they?" Serena averted his gaze and remained silent; she was reluctant to trust this stranger with her predicament.

"Listen, maybe I could drop you off somewhere." He paused. "Where do you live?"

"I was living with a friend in Brooklyn, but I can't go back there. I have to go somewhere else." Tears flooded her eyes but she tried not to blink, as she realized the trouble she was in. She had acted impulsively at the airport and now had put herself in a worse dilemma. The pain in her ankle was becoming unbearable. She lifted her left foot onto the seat, removed her sock and shoe, and massaged around her ankle, the tears running down her face.

"Oh boy," the man sighed. He turned his head toward the highway, started the engine and merged back into the flow of traffic. He looked at her in the rear view mirror. "I'm listening," he said kindly, afraid to upset her, hating for her to cry. Between quiet sobs, Serena decided to be truthful and told him how she came to be hiding in his van.

With empathy, Eric Reilly listened without interrupting. He had been raised by parents who taught him many golden rules, two of which were to love your neighbor as you love yourself, and be kind to others. As a teenager, he practiced kindness, had gone on missions' trips to tribal villages in South America, served thanksgiving meals to the homeless, and volunteered with Habitat for Humanity. Indeed, he had done his share of good deeds. Lately, he had no desire to become involved in other people's lives; he was simply too preoccupied with his own life. However, after hearing her story, he was moved to help this woman, who had nothing but the clothes on her back, was an illegal alien running from the law, and in pain from an injury to her foot.

Eric pulled the van into a driveway. "This is my parents' home," he said, "Wait here; I am going to ask my mother if you could stay here until we figure something out."

While he was gone, Serena weighed her options: She could get out and hop to the nearest train station and head back to Brooklyn, or she could trust this stranger to help her navigate the unknown. She was reaching for the handle of the passenger door when Eric appeared at the front door and hurried to the van. "I am taking you to a clinic to have your ankle examined; I called a friend who works there."

They rode in silence to the clinic, both preoccupied with their own thoughts of the situation. Eric was trying to make sense of what he was getting involved in, and confused about what was compelling him to do so. Serena was apprehensive about going back to Brooklyn, to the home of a stranger, and then what? Had she made her situation worse by becoming a fugitive from the law?

Chapter 11

E ric drove into the parking lot of a one-story, brown stone
building with the name Best Rehabilitation Clinic above
its main entrance. Quickly, he opened the door on the passenger side and offered Serena his hand. She took it and carefully
stepped down to the ground, grimacing from the pain pounding
in her left foot. She hopped on her right foot, holding onto his arm
for support, until Eric suddenly scooped her up into his arms and
carried her into the clinic. Once inside, they noticed two wheelchairs near the entrance. Eric gently placed her into one of the
wheelchairs and walked to the receptionist desk; there was no one
else in the waiting room.

As he spoke with the young woman at the reception desk, Serena finally got a chance to look at him without being noticed. He was
a tall man, with an athletic build, maybe in his late 20s, early 30s,
maybe of Irish or Italian heritage — she couldn't tell. All she knew
was his first name, but he was kind and she felt safe with him. While
he stood waiting, the door next to the reception desk opened and
a man wearing blue scrubs came out. He greeted Eric; they spoke
briefly, then they looked in Serena's direction. "Bring her in," he said.

She was wheeled down a hallway pass treatment rooms. They
followed the man into a room with an X-ray machine. As he busied
himself getting the machine ready, he asked, "So what happened?"

Serena did not answer. He stopped, came over to her and said, "I'm sorry, where are my manners? My name is Jon."

She shook his outstretched hand. "Hi," she smiled but avoided his gaze. "I was running, there was a hole in the pavement and I fell."

"Running, as in jogging?" he asked.

"No," was all Serena said.

"Well, let's take some X-ray pictures to see if any bone is broken." Eric, who had been asked to wait outside the room, was called back in after Jon took several pictures. "Give me a few minutes," Jon said, directing them to wait in one of the treatment rooms.

The silence was uncomfortable. Serena sat in the wheelchair and looked down at her bruised hands. Eric had picked up a *Sports Illustrated* from the magazine rack and was turning the pages. After a while, he said without looking up, "I told my mother that you are a friend, who is in a crisis situation, and need a place to stay until things are resolved." Serena could not look at him; she felt so ashamed. A long silence followed and then Jon came through the door.

"Well, fortunately, no broken bones, you have a Grade two sprain. You'll need to wear an ankle brace for about three weeks. For the next 48 hours, use an ice pack on it and keep your foot elevated." Jon moved around the room opening cupboards while he spoke. "You have to rest the ankle for it to heal; no weight bearing for about two weeks. I'll give you a pair of crutches to move around." He asked how tall she was and left the room. A few minutes later, he returned with a pair of crutches, which he adjusted and gave to Eric to hold while he put the brace on her now swollen foot. When he was finished, he gave Serena some sample packets and said, "Take Tylenol as needed for the pain. Call me if you have any concerns."

As they drove away from the clinic, Serena asked nervously, "Are you sure your mother won't mind a stranger coming to her home like this?" Eric did not answer immediately. When he stopped at the red light, he looked at her and said, "Well, before we go to my parent's home, why don't we find a place to talk. You can tell me the whole story, so I'll know what I am getting myself into. Besides, you're in no condition to go anywhere else right now."

Minutes later, he drove into the parking lot of a McDonald's restaurant and helped Serena out of the car. She positioned the crutches under her arms and hopped on one leg into the restaurant. While Eric ordered meals for both of them, she made her way to a corner table. While she waited for him to join her at the table, Serena thought of the circumstances in her life leading up to this moment and was uncertain how much more of her story she should disclose to Eric. But when he sat down across from her, she saw kindness in his eyes and felt that she could trust him.

So, she told him everything. Beginning with her illegal entry into the country, the painful disappointment at learning that Nick was married to someone else, her failed attempts with employment sponsorship, trying to obtain permanent resident status illegally, her arrest, detention and escape from deportation. She was relieved to get it all out. But sharing the events of her life made her sad; she saw herself as a failure and became teary eyed. Eric studied her face and listened without comments. When she had finished, she waited for him to say something; he appeared to be thinking about what to say. Finally, he smiled and said, "Well, for now the most important thing is that you need a place to recuperate, and once you can have both feet on the ground again, you can decide what to do." She was comforted by his kindness.

Eric gulped the last of his drink, leaned back in his seat, folded his arms and said, "I'll tell you my story so you'll understand why a 30-year-old man is living with his parents." He stared past her and remained silent for awhile. Then, he leaned forward with his forearms on the table, and looking down at his intertwined fingers, he said, "It's about 12 months since I moved back in with my parents. The house has a basement apartment, which gives me some privacy. My father has Alzheimer's; my mother insists on taking care of him by herself. But I help her as much as I can with errands and work around the house. My father doesn't know who I am anymore and that's been difficult for me."

He took a deep breath before continuing: "I moved in with them when my wife and I separated. I'm divorced now, my ex-wife and son still live in the home we had together. Our son Adam just turned four and is now in pre-school, which is a milestone for him. He was born 12 weeks premature, weighed only 2.5 pounds and had a lot of medical complications related to respiration and bleeding in the brain. He was in the neonatal intensive care nursery for eight weeks; my wife Jamie spent most of the eight weeks in the hospital with him. When he finally came home, he needed nursing care because he was still dependent on the ventilator. Then, shortly after he came home, he started having seizures, which led to more hospital stays and all kinds of neurological testing. To make a long story short, our son has cerebral palsy."

Serena noticed that Eric's eyes were filling with tears. He continued, "His diagnosis was a blow to us and Jamie had a very difficult time accepting it. She grieved the losses of the ideal life, the perfect family, the future. She was overwhelmed; and went through periods of rage, grief and depression. She became detached from everything and everyone — including me. The more I tried to get closer to her, the more she pulled away. I felt helpless. She became consumed with the care of Adam, and would not accept help from anyone. When I was at home, I felt her indifference toward me; so I buried myself in my work to cope."

Eric picked up the drink cup, shook the ice around and sipped on the straw. He continued, "By the time he was three and had overcome a lot of his medical issues, there was no place in Jamie's life for me. Her focus was only on Adam, his therapies, his doctor's appointments, and his equipment. The night she asked me for the divorce, it was the first time in a long time that we actually talked. She spoke about her intense guilt that she had caused our son to be disabled because of her hectic pace at work, and not allowing for adequate rest and nutrition. She complained of feeling isolated, because of the loss of her friends and career. I knew she was hurting, but I guess I didn't understand the depth of her pain. I moved out one month after she decided to end the marriage."

It was 4:00 p.m. when they left the restaurant. They were both silent on the drive back to Eric's parent's home. Eric could not believe how much he had opened up to Serena. Apart from his mother, he had never talked to anyone about the failure of his marriage. He knew that her prayers were sustaining him, as he dealt with the emotional rollercoaster his life had become. Initially, there were days he did not feel like facing the world, and she provided the words of encouragement he needed to hear.

They pulled into the driveway, and Eric sensed that Serena was nervous about meeting his mother. "My mother is the kindest person I know; stop worrying." He helped her out of the car and Mrs. Reilly met them at the door. "Hello dear." She kissed her son on the cheek and turned her attention to Serena; she looked at the boot cast and crutches. "You poor dear, come on into the kitchen; I'll fix you both something to eat."

"We had McDonald's, mom," Eric said as they followed her into the kitchen.

"Well, how about some tea or hot chocolate?" She looked at Serena.

"Hot chocolate would be nice, thank you."

Mrs. Reilly busied herself with the kettle, cups and getting the hot chocolate ready as Eric and Serena sat at the table.

"Is Dad asleep?" Eric asked his mother.

"He is in his chair in the living room dozing. He takes several naps during the day and seldom sleeps through the night; he is usually up and restless by 11." She placed the cups and a plate of oatmeal raisin cookies on the table. Then, tapping Serena on the shoulder, she added, "If you hear any commotion during the night, it's me trying to get Mr. Reilly back to bed." Before long, they were drinking hot chocolate and eating cookies like three friends in Mrs. Reilly's country kitchen. She made them laugh as she told Serena stories about her Italian heritage, after Serena commented on the spicy aroma in the kitchen.

Mrs. Reilly was first to get up from the table. "Come, dear, let me show you to your room. I put fresh linens on the bed. You'll be in Melissa's bedroom; it's just the way she left it when she moved to California two years ago."

Serena stood up; looking in her purse for the packets of Tylenol the therapist had given her. Eric anticipated her need and quickly got her a glass of water. She swallowed two pills, hoping to ease the throbbing pain in her left foot. Climbing up the stairs with the crutches was difficult at first, but she slowly made it up without losing her balance. Once in the bedroom, Mrs. Reilly opened the closet door. "You are about the same size as my daughter; feel free to use the clothing in here," she opened the dresser drawers, "and in here." She moved items around. "Melissa left most of her clothing, and I haven't had time to take them to the Salvation Army; so they are yours, whatever you need."

"Thank you," Serena whispered, trying to keep away the tears, overwhelmed by the kindness of these strangers.

As Mrs. Reilly was about to leave the room, she halted, "Oh dear, you are going to need some undergarments and toiletries, aren't you?" She frowned, then her face lit up, "No worries, I'll pick some up for you tomorrow; I'll make a quick run to the store while Mr. Reilly is asleep. Good night, my dear, pleasant dreams."

In the days following her arrival at the Reilly's, Serena settled into the routine of the home and marveled everyday at the generosity of the family. She watched Mrs. Reilly lovingly care for her husband, with patience and kindness that she had never witnessed before. She enjoyed talking to Mrs. Reilly and listening to her words of wisdom.

"*Earthly love may fail us, my dear, but God's love is eternal, unchanging.*" She said when Serena told her about Nick and the promises that were broken.

On a beautiful sunny late afternoon, Serena put on one of the coats she found in the bedroom closet and ventured out into the backyard. She sat on one of the wicker chairs around the outdoor table enjoying the cool and tender breeze of spring. The backyard was in the shape of a square and enclosed by a tall wooden privacy fence. The cement patio, made up of red and tan cement tiles formed a checker board pattern and took up most of the land space. In the space between the cement patio and the fence was a variety of rose bushes, tulips, and other flower plants. Butterflies of all colors and sizes fluttered about, bees floated around the bright yellow marigolds and dandelions. Serena was enjoying the peacefulness of the moment. Belize has the most beautiful butterflies she thought, as she remembered her childhood days, running through the corn fields with Valerie, trying to catch the butterflies with the prettiest colors.

"Hey!" She hadn't heard Eric approaching. He looked down at her, smiling. "Shouldn't you be keeping that foot elevated?" Before she could answer, he lifted her foot and placed it on the nearby chair. "How are you?"

"Getting better every day" Serena smiled. "It is less painful today than it was yesterday."

He looked at her foot. "The swelling has gone down." Eric sat in the chair opposite her. "What are you reading?" he asked, noticing the closed book in her lap.

Serena picked up the book. "The Cross and the Switchblade, your mom gave it to me."

"Ah, I read it years ago myself." There was a long pause, until Serena broke the silence.

"Your mom is a very nice lady, I really like her and I am learning a lot from her."

Eric looked down at the ground and declared, "My mom is a Titus 2 woman." He looked up and off into the distance. "That's the kind of woman I wanted to marry." He smiled.

"She talks a lot about past involvement in church ministries."

"Yes, men's ministry, women's ministry, support groups, prayer groups, you name it, they were involved in it. My dad was a deacon for years; he also led praise and worship on Sundays." Eric paused, sat back in the chair and crossed his legs. "My sister and I were involved in youth programs, went on missions' trips, youth camps, and did a lot of community volunteering. I played the guitar in the youth praise and worship band; I had a real commitment then."

"What changed for you?"

Eric sighed, looked at Serena and said, "That's a good question. I remember that I started to lose my faith when I was in college." He sighed again. "I wish I could answer that question." And with that, he stood up and said, "I am going to take my son to dinner and a Disney movie. It's not my night to have him, but we pleaded and his mother is allowing us to hang out together for a few hours." His expression changed to joy and anticipation. He tapped Serena on the shoulder, "See you later kiddo."

Shortly after Eric left, Serena rose carefully, positioned the crutches under her arm pits and made her way indoors. She was about to climb the stairs to the bedroom, when she heard Mrs. Reilly reading out loud in the family room. She looked in and saw that Mr. Reilly was lying on the sofa, his eyes were closed and he looked relaxed. Mrs. Reilly was sitting on a chair next to his head reading to him from the Bible. She looked up and motioned Serena to join them.

"He likes it when I read to him from the Bible; it calms him." She rubbed his head and continued reading about Joseph and the emotional reunion with his brothers, after he revealed himself to them in the land of Egypt. Mr. Reilly opened his eyes, looked at his wife and smiled while she read. He was snoring softly by the time she ended the chapter. She closed the Bible gently, laid it on the coffee table, rose quietly and beckoned Serena to follow her; they went into the kitchen. As she busied herself making tea, she said, "One of his favorite things to do at church was teaching Bible study groups. Now his mind is in a fog. He recognizes the scriptures though, whenever I read to him, it's like he finds rest and peace in the word." She placed a cup of tea and a plate of chocolate chip cookies in front of Serena and sat opposite her with the same.

"What about you, Mrs. Reilly?" Serena asked. "Do you miss going to church?"

"I do," She responded. There was sadness in her eyes. "He doesn't know Eric as his son anymore, and he becomes anxious and agitated when anyone else is with him; he is calm and contented when I am with him." As Mrs. Reilly looked down and stirred her tea, lost in her own thoughts for a moment, Serena studied her. She was a very special lady who spent most of her time during the day taking care of her husband's needs. Her eyes were puffy and tired from lack of a good night sleep because he got out of the bed several times during the night. Mr. Reilly could no longer feed, bath or dress himself; he was totally dependent and Mrs. Reilly never complained. Serena wanted to help her.

"I can take care of Mr. Reilly while you attend church." She offered. "He seems to tolerate me being here, and I would be happy to do anything to help; you have been very kind and generous to me."

Mrs. Reilly reached out and held Serena's hand. "That would be wonderful dear," she beamed. "You're right; I just realized that he does not seem to mind having you around."

Chapter 12

At the end of her second week with the Reilly's, Serena was eager to meet Eric's son Adam, who was visiting for the weekend. When Eric left to pick him up, she sat at the kitchen table and waited reading from a copy of the Readers Digest. Then she remembered Eric's comment about his mother being a Titus two woman, and was curious to know what he meant, so she picked up the bible left on the table by Mrs. Reilly and began to read the second chapter of Titus. She read the entire chapter and was about to read it again when she heard Eric's car pull into the driveway. Mrs. Reilly had taken Mr. Reilly upstairs and was getting him ready for bed. After a lot of commotion at the front door, they came into the kitchen, both with big smiles on their faces, Eric pushing Adam in a stroller and carrying a duffle bag slung over his shoulder.

"Here he is," Eric announced proudly. "Adam, say hi to my friend Serena."

Adam looked at Serena above the rim of his glasses. He took a deep breath and exhaled, "Hi." Serena was immediately smitten. He was a beautiful little boy with thick, unruly blonde curls, a round face, and deep sea blue eyes behind thin, black metal frame glasses.

She leaned towards him, "Hi, Adam, it's nice to finally meet you; your grandma and dad told me all about you." He smiled again, but looked down at the floor.

"Come now, buddy, you're not shy," Eric said tousling his son's hair. "Grandma made your favorite, macaroni and cheese." Adam looked up at his father and smiled, "Are you ready to eat?"

Eric lifted Adam out of the stroller and put him in a special chair with side supports; it had been in a corner of the kitchen. He put the food in a special bowl with a suction ring on the bottom. "Adam is learning to feed himself," he said proudly. Serena looked admirably at the two, noticing that Adam's grasp on the handle of the spoon was weak. He spilled some, but he was feeding himself. Eric saw Serena's attempts to assist him and said, "He has to do it by himself, because big boys feed themselves."

Adam shook his head, "yes," then smiled at Serena, his mouth stuffed with macaroni and cheese.

Eric fixed himself a plate and joined them at the table. Just then, Mrs. Reilly came into the kitchen. She grinned widely as she walked over to Adam and said, "Is that my favorite grandson?" Adam's face light up. She kissed him on the head and tousled his hair.

That evening, a loving relationship between Serena and Adam began. She looked forward to the weekends he visited. The more time she spent with Adam, helping Eric entertain him, the more she realized how much she missed her own son, and perhaps Adam was filling the void in her heart.

❦ ❦

Serena was dreaming about Benjamin: He was pulling wild flowers off their stems in the open field at the back of the house, and bringing them to her where she sat on a large rock chewing on sugar cane stalks. There was a feeling of peace and contentment in the field as she watched him talking to himself, his hands busy at work. The dream felt so real. When the knock on her bedroom door woke her up; she was disappointed that it was not. "Serena, Serena!" Mrs. Reilly's voice was urgent.

She sprang off the bed and opened the bedroom door. "Serena, Mr. Reilly is nowhere in the house! I can't find him!" Mrs. Reilly was wearing her bathrobe, her hair was dripping wet and she had the most frantic look on her face. "He was lying on the bed when I went into the shower. I came out and he was gone. I have looked all over the house." While Mrs. Reilly was talking, Serena quickly put on sweat pants, sneakers and pulled her hair back in a ponytail.

"Don't worry," she reassured Mrs. Reilly, "he couldn't have góne too far; I'll look for him."

"I'll call 9-1-1," Mrs. Reilly said as she began to walk back toward her bedroom.

"No!" Serena stopped on her way down the stairs. "Don't call yet; I'll look for him first." She immediately thought of the implications of having the police involved.

Serena saw that the front door was only slightly ajar, not easily noticed. She stepped outside pulling the door shut behind her, and ran to the bottom of the driveway, looking up and down the street. It was 7:30 and the morning air was cold. She needed a sweater, but there was no time to go back into the house. As she pondered briefly whether to go left or right, she whispered a prayer to find Mr. Reilly quickly, remembering another time when she prayed in her search for Zachary. She turned left toward Bradford Street, quickening her pace, and looking into driveways as she hurried down the street. On either side of the street, small groups of children were walking to the elementary school at the corner of Bradford and Fletcher streets.

On Bradford Street she turned left toward the school; she was already a block away from the house and there was no sign of Mr. Reilly. The neighborhood was mostly residential, but the streets were busy with school buses and cars in the early morning and afternoon. Serena was halfway up the block on Bradford when she noticed a commotion up ahead. A group of kids were gathered at the curb near the cross walk, laughing and restlessly moving around. She walked faster, and as she got closer, she saw the crossing guard, a short, stocky woman; holding on to Mr. Reilly's arm and pulling him back to the curb to prevent him from crossing the street. He was pulling away from her; she lost her grip on his arm, but grabbed the back of his pajama shirt. The children laughed again.

Serena got to the curb just as Mr. Reilly wiggled himself free and headed for the middle of the street. She ran and got in front of him and put her hands on his chest to stop his forward momentum. She then held his forearms, but he began to struggle, his eyes wild with fear. "Mr. Reilly," Serena said in a firm voice. He looked at her face then. "Rose is waiting for you at home." He recognized her and stopped resisting, allowing her to hold his hand and guide him back to the sidewalk. When they were safely away from the street, Serena looked at him, his face grimaced with confusion and anxiety. She spoke gently to him. "You're okay now; I'll take you home to Rose." He began to cry as she led him to a low wall where they sat together. She put her arm around his broad shoulder, and he held onto her other hand like a frightened child.

A few minutes later, his whimpering stopped and he became calm. The crossing guard came over to where they were sitting. "Thank you," Serena said to her. She smiled, and looking at Mr. Reilly, said, "I could tell that something was wrong with him, dressed liked that, trying to cross a busy street. I had to stop him before he got hurt."

The woman returned to her spot at the curb. Only then did Serena realize that Mr. Reilly had no slippers on, and was shivering wearing only thin cotton pajamas and socks. It had been about 15 minutes since she left the house; they needed to get back soon, before Mrs. Reilly called 9-1-1. He was still anxious and held her hand tightly. She could not leave him to find a phone to call the house, and he was in no condition to walk the distance back. Suddenly, she became aware of the pain in her left ankle.

"Do you need some help?" Serena looked around and saw a young woman with a concerned look on her face. "I was parking my car and saw what was happening; I am a teacher at the school."

"I have to get him home right away, his wife is worried, but I don't think he can walk back to the house; he is pretty shaken up."

"I'll drive you," she offered. She went back to her car and pulled up to the curb in front of them. A few minutes later, Serena was helping Mr. Reilly out of the car and up the driveway.

He was visibly exhausted, but the joy on his face as his wife embraced him brought tears to Serena's eyes. Mrs. Reilly hugged and kissed her, "Thank you my dear. I was so worried; he's never done anything like this before." She held her husband's hand, smiling now. "Come along, road runner, I'll make you a big breakfast." She led her husband to the kitchen.

🐝🐝

As the days passed, Serena felt as if she had always been there at the Reilly's. Her ankle was better, but she had no idea what her next move should be. When she had called Emma at the bank, who was shocked at her escape from deportation, she had advised her not to come back to the apartment in case the INS was watching and waiting for her to show up there.

She had settled into a routine helping Mrs. Reilly with the housework, and they enjoyed each other's company. Eric was home from work around 5:30 p.m. two to three days a week to help his mother. Serena accompanied him several times when he did the food shopping, she also helped him with the yard work and chores around the house. Occasionally when Eric wanted to go to the movies, he invited her along, and he took her out for Chinese food a few times. They laughed a lot together about silly things, but never talked about her situation or what she should do now that her ankle had healed.

It was almost three months since Mrs. Reilly had taken her in, and she had settled into a state of contentment in spite of the uncertainty. Then, one evening while cleaning the kitchen, she was suddenly overwhelmed with sadness. She turned off the lights in the kitchen and decided to go upstairs to her bedroom; she needed to spend some time thinking about her limited options and what to do next. Serena paused at the doorway of the living room to say goodnight, but Mrs. Reilly motioned with her hand for her to come in. She had been reading to Mr. Reilly as he lay on the sofa, his eyes closed, a peaceful look on his face. She closed the Bible and whispered, "I am going to play his favorite hymn; watch what happens."

The music started, and then a choir began to sing. Serena had never heard that hymn before, and she was struck by the poignancy of the words and the beauty of the melody:

"When peace, like a river, attendeth my way, when sorrows like sea billows roll: whatever my lot, thou has taught me to say, It is well; it is well, with my soul..."

Serena watched intently as Mr. Reilly opened his eyes and smiled. He sat up slowly, then stood up, he held his tall six foot frame upright. The choir was now singing the chorus:

"It is well, with my soul, it is well, it is well, with my soul."

Suddenly, he began moving his arms like a choir conductor. She had never seen him so alert and animated. Mrs. Reilly, standing next to the record player was laughing and clapping her hands. Serena focused on the words as she stared at Mr. Reilly.

"And Lord, haste the day when my faith shall be sight, the clouds be rolled back as a scroll, the trump shall resound, and the Lord shall descend, even so, it is well with my soul."

Mr. Reilly closed his eyes and turned his face upward, moving his arms vigorously until the song ended. Mrs. Reilly walked over to him, hugged and kissed him on the lips. They stared at each other for a moment and he smiled.

Tears blurred Serena's vision. "It has always been his favorite hymn," Mrs. Reilly said as she helped her husband to sit back down on the sofa. "I have a book of all the old hymns and the story behind them." She walked over to the bookshelf, "Here it is, read the story of the man who wrote this song." She turned to Mr. Reilly and said, "Come along, my charming Irishman, let's get you to bed."

Now alone in the living room, Serena settled in the arm chair next to the table lamp and read the story of Horatio G. Spafford, the man who penned the words, *"It is well with my soul."* Minutes later, she closed the book, buried her face in her tee-shirt and wept quietly. She did not know how to have faith and peace in the midst of life's turmoil. That night in her bed Serena prayed, telling God about her painful disappointments since leaving home, her many mistakes, her inability to have clear guidance in her life, and the guilt of leaving Benjamin behind. She asked God to help her find her path through life with clear directions on what to do next. When she was finished praying the overwhelming sadness she had felt earlier was gone; Serena had restful sleep that night.

Chapter 13

Under the wisdom and guidance of Mrs. Reilly during their daily interactions, Serena began to discover spiritual strength and confidence. She was now at peace about repairing countless mistakes. Meanwhile, more and more, she looked forward to the weekends that Adam spent with his dad, her love for the precious child growing each time she saw him. They played games on the floor and colored pictures with crayons, and she read him stories, usually while Eric was helping his mother with errands or chores around the house. One weekend, she eagerly anticipated Adam's arrival, because he was excited about learning to walk with a posterior Kaye walker.

❦ ❦

As she waited upstairs in her bedroom she thought about the day Adam got his walker. Eric had invited her to join them when he took Adam to the clinic to try the walker for the first time. "You need to have a follow-up visit about your ankle anyway," he had said. She was happy to go along. The physical therapist examined her ankle, there was no pain as he checked the range of motion in the joint and he declared that she had healed well. "No more running on bad roads, unless someone is chasing you," he told her, smiling. Eric looked at Serena knowingly and they all laughed.

Then, the therapist picked Adam up out of his wheelchair and carried him to the parallel bars, where he assisted him to hold onto the bars, then prompted him to walk forward. With rigid movements in his legs, he struggled to lift his feet to clear the surface, but he persisted as his father cheered him on. After a rest break, the therapist adjusted the walker to match Adam's height and said, "Okay Adam, let's try the walker." He positioned Adam's hands on the handle bars and gently pulled the walker forward to initiate the movement. His face beaming with excitement, Adam smiled, looked at his father, then at Serena.

The therapist sat on a rolling stool in front of him and gently pulled the walker forward. Adam lifted his right foot and cleared the surface, but lifting his left foot required more effort; the therapist had described it as high muscle tone and tightness on his left involved side. After a few trying steps, he collapsed to the floor on his knees. Eric, Serena noticed, was fighting the impulse to go to him and pick him up. The therapist helped him to get up and positioned his hands on the walker again. Eric walked over, kissed him on the forehead and said, "You're doing great, buddy. Everyone falls a few times when they are learning to walk."

The remainder of the session went well, with Adam slowly taking small steps forward, and pulling the walker behind him. "Don't forget he needs to practice this every day to gain strength in his legs and to work on his balance and coordination. If he seems a bit unstable, we could add some weight to the walker. Call me with any questions or concerns."

Eric's eyes were filling with tears as he hugged the therapist and said, "Thanks, man."

❦❦ ❦❦

Serena heard when they came in and hurried downstairs. Adam was all smiles when he saw her. The love and adoration he and Serena shared was especially poignant today.

"Hi Ce," he said, beaming. Adam had to take a deep breath before he spoke, and he was limited to two to three words at a time. While Eric retrieved Adam's overnight bag, walker, story books and toys from the car, Serena wheeled him into the kitchen, where his grandmother was feeding breakfast to his grandfather. "Here is my favorite grandson in the whole wide world," Mrs. Reilly proudly proclaimed, the mantra that she used each time she saw him, right before she kissed him on the forehead and tousled his curly blonde hair.

The phone rang shortly after they arrived and Eric had to leave for an emergency at work. He asked Serena if she would take care of Adam until he returned, since Mrs. Reilly had already planned to go food shopping and to do a few errands. In recent weeks, Mrs. Reilly had been able to leave the house because Mr. Reilly was no longer anxious; he felt safe with Serena since that scary morning when she rescued him from the street. Occasionally, his eyes even twinkled when she sat with him at the table.

After Serena supervised Adam with his breakfast, and Mrs. Reilly left, the three of them sat in the living room. Mr. Reilly sat resting his head on the back of the chair, his eyes closed, he looked peaceful and content. She could tell when he fell asleep from his slow, steady breathing. Adam sat next to her on the sofa, watching his Saturday morning lineup of cartoons, as she folded a load of laundry. It was peaceful being there with this family that made no demands and accepted her; she felt nurtured and safe. The nights were no longer difficult, like those in the past when she'd lay awake with troubling thoughts of how hard life was and of her limited options to make it better. It was noon by the time she had finished the three loads of laundry and Mrs. Reilly returned. While Serena put the groceries away, Mrs. Reilly prepared lunch. "How were the boys, did they behave for you?" she asked.

"They were on their best behavior. Adam fell asleep on the sofa a short while ago."

"Good, let them sleep; we'll have a quiet lunch together before they wake up."

She walked over and put her arms around Serena. "It is so good to get out to do the errands myself; thanks dear." She kissed her on the cheek. Mrs. Reilly was very affectionate, unlike her aunt Julia.

After lunch, Serena decided to help Adam practice walking in the back yard. Eric was eager for him to walk and often took him to the nearby park, or the sidewalk in front of the house to practice. First, she took the walker outside, then carried Adam and placed him on a chair as she moved the patio furniture to one side, clearing a path the length of the yard from the fence to the kitchen door. Then, she stood him up, placed his hands on the handles, and positioned herself in front of him. Adam was a bit unsteady on his feet and struggled to move even slightly forward. Serena placed her hands over his and gently pulled him forward. He smiled, and started to gain momentum. She backed away, but stayed close enough to catch him if he lost his balance.

"Good boy, you're doing it!" She clapped her hands and started to sing, "*Those feet are made for walking, and that's just what they'll do, and one of these days those feet are gonna walk...........*" Serena stopped abruptly, noticing that Adam was suddenly no longer moving and was quite rigid, his eyes twitching and rolling back. She reached forward and caught him just as he slumped toward the ground. With her arms around his upper body, she felt him shaking. She gathered him in her arms, picked him up and rushed to the back door, banging on it with her foot and calling out to Mrs. Reilly, who was still in the kitchen. "Oh, dear God, he is having a seizure!" she exclaimed frantically. "Lay him on the big sofa and stay with him, please; I'll call 9-1-1."

The paramedics arrived in seven minutes, and by then Adam's convulsions were violent. One paramedic gave him an injection, while the other covered his mouth and nose with an oxygen mask. "We'll have to take him in," one of them said matter of fact to Mrs. Reilly.

"Oh, Serena," Mrs. Reilly said nervously, "I can't leave Mr. Reilly; can you please go to the hospital? I'll call his mother and Eric right away." Without hesitation, Serena climbed into the back of the ambulance, the ear-piercing siren blasting as it sped down the street. The paramedic checked Adam's pulse, shined a small light into his eyes and wrote on a clipboard. The convulsions had stopped; now he appeared unresponsive. Serena covered her mouth with her hands and tried desperately to hold back the gush of tears, as she stared at him.

Without looking up at her, the woman asked, "Does he have a history of seizures? Is he taking seizure medications?"

"I don't know, but I have seen his father give him medication in the evenings."

Looking up, she asked, "Are you his babysitter?"

"No, ma'am, I'm just a friend of the family."

"What was he doing when he started having the seizure?"

"He was in the back yard with me practicing to walk with a walker."

She wanted to ask if Adam could die from the seizure, but was afraid to hear the answer. So she just sat still, stoically staring at him, silently praying for a miracle.

When the ambulance stopped at the entrance of the emergency room, the driver quickly jumped out, opened the back door, and in a well-choreographed set of movements, the two of them had Adam out and wheeled him into the emergency room. Serena followed close behind them. One of the paramedics and a nurse hurriedly exchanged information. "Take him into triage," the nurse commanded.

"Can I go in with him?" Serena asked the nurse.

She responded tersely, "Where are his parents?"

Serena paused, then replied, "I'm sure they will be here soon."

"Only his parents will be allowed back there; you should wait in the waiting area."

Serena walked away from the nurses' station, and looked around for a water fountain, all the while praying silently that Adam would be alright. She was walking back to the waiting area when she saw a woman frantically running through the emergency room; she almost collided with a man walking away from the nurses' station.

"Excuse me," she panted. "My son was brought in here a short while ago." She took a deep breath. "His name is Adam Reilly."

"He is in triage, Room five, through those doors, I need his......." The woman bolted through the double doors before the nurse could finish her sentence.

The waiting room was crowded; Serena hadn't noticed that when she followed the paramedics in. She managed to find a seat between an older man who appeared to be intoxicated with bruises decorating his face, and a young man cradling his left arm with his right, he was grimacing in pain. A spattering of mothers gently held young children who were either coughing or crying. Serena sat with her elbows on her knees and covered her face with her hands to avoid looking at the chaos around her. She had no idea how much time had passed.

"Serena." Someone touched her shoulder. She looked up and saw Eric standing over her.

"Hi," she said as she stood up, and walked with him toward the nurses' station.

"Do you know where Adam is?"

"I heard the nurse say triage Room five when your wife came in; it's through those doors." She pointed to the double doors.

"Thank you for being here." Eric put his arms around Serena, kissed her on the forehead and darted behind the doors.

She returned to the waiting room. About 30 minutes passed; she got up to move around and saw Eric and his ex wife at the opposite end of the hall engaging in what seemed like a heated argument. Her hand gestures and body language were angry. Then, with a look of defeat, Eric began walking back toward the waiting area, and Jaime headed back toward the double doors.

"I'll drive you back to the house now," he said solemnly to Serena, and she followed him to his car. He was quiet and appeared to be holding in mounds of emotions. She was quiet, too, respecting his need to be alone with his thoughts.

As they pulled into the driveway, he said, "Tell my mom Adam is going to be fine, they are keeping him for observation and want to run some more tests. I'm going back to the hospital; I'll be home later."

After Serena updated Mrs. Reilly, the relieved grandmother put both hands on her chest, sighed and said, "Whew, I have been so worried."

Later that evening, after Eric had returned and was eating dinner in the kitchen, Serena sat across from him at the table, anxiously listening to an update on Adam. "He is awake and alert now. They did blood work, and plan to increase his seizure medication dosage." Eric explained. Then suddenly exasperated, Eric put his fork down and said sullenly, "Jamie said some really awful things to me. I don't think that my going to work and leaving him brought on his seizure. She always seems to know exactly what to say to hurt me." He put his head in his hands as tears trickled down the sides of his face. Serena moved to the chair closest to him. "She is worried and anxious about Adam; people say mean things when they are upset. You are a good father, and she knows that."

She took one of his hands and held it with both of hers, and when Eric looked up at her, he wept uncontrollably. She reached over and cradled his head on her shoulder and put her arms around him. "It's not your fault; he would have had the seizure whether you were here or not." He took both her hands in his, stared into her eyes and said, "Thank you for being here."

❧ ☙

After that emotional moment together, Serena went back up to bed, but could not fall asleep. The events of the day had left her emotionally drained and watching Eric fall apart tonight left her sad. She contemplated how, since leaving Belize, she had witnessed and experienced a series of trials and tragedies. She sat up, turned on the lamp on the night table, reached for the clock radio and moved the dial slowly, trying to find the radio station Mrs. Reilly listened to, that played inspirational songs and old hymns. She needed to listen to something soothing to calm the growing anxiety inside her. Serena stopped turning the dial when an announcer said, "Here is a song by the Grammy winning song writer and performer, Andrae Crouch, 'Through It All.'"

Serena placed the radio back on the night stand and was about to lay down, when the first words of the song grabbed her attention. She sat motionless; her eyes closed, and listened.

I've had many tears and sorrows, I've had questions for tomorrow, there've been times I didn't know right from wrong, but in every situation, God gave blessed consolation that my trials come to only make me strong.

Through it all, through it all, I've learned to trust in Jesus, I've learned to trust in God:

Through it all, through it all, I've learned to depend upon his word.

I've been to lots of places, and I've seen a lot of faces, there've been times I felt so all alone; But in my lonely hours, yes, those precious lonely hours, Jesus let me know that I was his own.

I thank God for the mountains, and I thank him for the valleys, I thank him for the storms He brought me through, for if I'd never had a problem, I wouldn't know that he could solve them, I'd never know what faith in God could do."

By the time the song ended, tears were flowing down her face. *The tears, the sorrows, the storms, the mountains and the valleys, she had been through it all. She had questions for tomorrow; for her future and that of her son.* She grieved the fact that she did not have an earthly mother and father, but she knew now that she had a heavenly Father who loved her and created her for a purpose. Mrs. Reilly had said, *"Trust in the Lord with all your heart and lean not on your own understandings, in all your ways acknowledge him and he shall direct your path."*

She found a sense of peace when she finally lay down. It was a peace she had never felt before, and as she was drifting off to sleep she knew what her next move should be.

Serena awoke the next morning joyous, as if a burden had been lifted. While having breakfast with Mrs. Reilly, she told her about her prayer, the sense of peace that came over her and her decision to return home to Belize. Mrs. Reilly reached for her hand across the table, looked into her eyes and said, "We are going to miss you something awful; it's been so good having you here. You've been such a help to me and Eric, but you are doing the right thing, my dear." Tears weld up in both their eyes. "Just learn to trust God with everything in your life."

They were both mopping the tears from their eyes and smiling, when the doorbell rang. Mrs. Reilly sprang to her feet and went to answer it. "Jamie my dear, what a pleasant surprise, is everything okay with Adam?" Serena remained seated at the table almost dreading meeting Eric's wife after witnessing the confrontation at the hospital and seeing the pain it had caused Eric.

"He is doing better; the doctor plans to discharge him tomorrow if he continues to be seizure free."

"Good, come on in, have some coffee."

"Thanks, but I can't stay, I came to see Eric. Is he here?"

"No, dear, he already left for work, but he plans to get off early to go to the hospital."

Serena's heart began to beat faster as she heard their footsteps approaching the kitchen. She stood up when Jamie entered.

"Hi, you must be Ce. Adam mentions your name a lot," Jamie said, extending her hand. Serena smiled and shook her hand. She was a bit intimidated by Jamie's beauty. Adam got his curly blonde hair and blue eyes from his mother she thought as Jamie continued, looking directly at her. "I am so sorry about the way I overreacted last night. I had no right to speak to Eric the way I did." She paused, and then continued, "The truth is, I was the one at fault. My parents came to visit on Thursday night, we went out to dinner, they stayed with us overnight and I forgot to give Adam his medication. We went out again on Friday night, and then they left to go back to New York and again I forgot to give him his nightly dose. When they did his blood work at the hospital last night and saw how low his levels were, I remembered the missed doses. But when Eric came back to the hospital, I was too ashamed to say anything to him then."

Jamie looked away, because tears were now overflowing her eyes. Mrs. Reilly stepped forward and embraced her. "Eric will be at the hospital later; you can tell him then. The most important thing is that Adam is going to be fine."

As Jamie dried her eyes, she looked at Serena again and said, "Adam really likes you; he tries to tell me about you when he comes home. Thank you for all you do for him."

Later that morning, Serena called Emma at the bank to let her know of her plans, and she began to take the necessary steps for the journey home.

Chapter 14

The next morning, Eric drove Serena to the station to take the train to Manhattan. After he parked the car along the curb at the entrance of the train station, she was reluctant to get out. When their eyes met, Eric smiled and said, "Hope everything goes well today." He has such a reassuring smile, she thought.

"Thank you, I appreciate everything you have done for me." For a long while, they stared at each other.

Eric finally broke the silence. "I'll be here around 5:30 to pick you up."

She got out of the car and walked toward the big glass doors. Turning around, she waved at him and entered the station.

As she purchased her ticket, the agent announced that the train to New York would be about 10 minutes late. Serena walked outside onto the platform to wait, but the cotton jacket she was wearing wasn't warm enough to withstand the windy, chilly air. Returning inside the station, she sat down and immediately recalled her conversation with Eric the night before. He had been a bit melancholy for two days because of the incident with Adam and the war of words with his wife. Although Jamie had apologized to him, her words and actions had opened old wounds. When Serena told him about her decision to return home to Belize, his eyes narrowed and the sadness on his face became more intense. He listened to her reasoning and agreed that it was the right decision, but she felt as if she had unearthed something inside of him. After their conversation, she became restless, her feelings toward Eric suddenly more apparent to her.

The train pulled into the station screeching loudly. Serena jumped to her feet and boarded. She walked through the cars until she spotted an unoccupied window seat. By the time she sat down, the train was gliding out of the station. She was anxious about today, her mind filled with unrealistic fears about being caught and imprisoned, this time for being a fugitive from the law. She was meeting Emma in Manhattan. Together, they were going to the Belize embassy, where Serena would apply for a new passport. Emma had convinced her in a phone conversation to replace her passport. Serena also realized that upon arrival in Belize, she would need to show documentation to prove that she was a citizen.

After the train pulled into Penn Station, Serena made her way up the escalators and through the station, following the arrows to the main entrance and the street. It was mid morning and less busy than during rush hour. As planned, Emma was waiting just outside the main entrance door. Serena saw her first through the glass doors; she had a suitcase on the ground next to her. They embraced each other, eyes overflowing with tears of joy.

"It's so good to see you," Emma said as they finally pulled apart. "You look great, gained a pound or two, yes?" Emma joked.

Serena laughed. "Yes, at least four or five. I've been feasting on delicious Italian meals."

Emma's expression became serious, as she held both of Serena's hands, looked her in the eyes and said, "You are doing the right thing, Serena. If you remain in this country illegally, you will not be able to take advantage of opportunities to advance your life, you will have to lie to get by, and more importantly you want to be able to raise your son."

"I know," Serena responded quietly.

Emma grabbed the handle of the suitcase and said, "Let's get a taxi cab."

The small waiting room in the embassy was not crowded as she had feared, but Serena was reluctant to go in, she paused at the entrance and looked at every person; she didn't recognize anyone. Emma went up to the counter, took a number and asked for a passport application. Together, they sat in the far corner of the room. Serena put the clipboard on her lap and filled out the application. She looked up and whispered to Emma, "They want a reason why I am applying for a new passport."

Emma thought for a minute and then whispered, "Original passport lost." Serena stared at her. "Well, technically it was lost in the possession of a con artist." Serena smiled and continued to complete the form, listing the Reilly's address as her mailing address.

"Did you get passport pictures?" Emma asked suddenly as if she just had a revelation.

"Yes, Eric took me to K-Mart yesterday and I got it done there."

The two friends were so happy to be together, quietly swapping stories, that they were oblivious to everyone else in the waiting room. Serena told Emma about Mr. and Mrs. Reilly, their son Eric and his son Adam. Emma talked about work, school and the Grenadian guy she was dating; he played the piano for worship at a church she started attending after Serena left. Emma wanted details of her escape at the airport, and about the sudden sparkle in her eyes when she spoke about Eric, but decided to wait to chat during lunch when they didn't have to whisper. Meanwhile, people shuffled in and out of the room. When it was Serena's turn at the counter, the woman looked over her application, stapled the two photos to it, asked for the $25 fee and told her that the passport would be mailed to her in five to seven business days. It was that simple, surprisingly.

They left the embassy and Emma suggested Charlie's Restaurant across the street for lunch. After they were seated and had given the waitress their orders, they resumed their conversation. Emma listened intently to details of Serena's escape at the airport, her injury and life with the Reillys, her facial expressions reflecting her amazement. The waitress placed the food in front of them, and it sat there. Serena did not want to break the momentum of the story, and Emma was too intrigued to break from listening. When the waitress came back to their table and asked, "Is everything Okay?" they realized that they hadn't touched their food. Between bites, Emma told Serena about the visit she had from the same two INS officers the evening of the day she had escaped at the airport. "I wasn't worried about the interrogation as much as I was about your well-being. I think they were embarrassed by how easily you were able to get away. So they may have been watching my apartment for a while waiting to see if you would show up. It's good that you we able to call me at work."

Emma reached into her handbag. "Before I forget, here is all the money from the joint account we had together. I withdrew $100 each month for the past three months, and sent it to your aunt with brief letters as if they were from you." She handed Serena a thick brown envelope, sealed with tape and bound with a large rubber band. Emma handed her another piece of paper. "This is information on the airlines flying to Belize. Call and make arrangements on the phone or use a local travel agency in Connecticut to make the arrangements for you." She looked down and tapped the suitcase. "This is only half of your clothing and shoes; I packed the remainder of your things in a large box, and I will mail it to you later."

They continued to eat and enjoy their time together. Emma noticed that Serena's face lit up when she talked about Mrs. Reilly. She described how conversations with Mrs. Reilly helped her to grow spiritually, with a deeper understanding of what it means to have a relationship with God, and how she found joy in the day to day routines in that home. After a pause between them, Emma said, "So, it sounds like Eric is a really nice guy." Serena smiled, lowered her head, and twirled a French fry in a glob of ketchup on her plate. When she didn't reply, Emma asked, "Are you completely over Nick?" When Serena looked up, she noticed that Emma gazed toward the entrance of the restaurant. She followed Emma's gaze and there, standing inside the doorway looking around, was Nick. Emma lifted her hand and waved; he saw them. Serena stared in disbelief as he approached, and the same wave of nausea she felt that day at his apartment came over her. She wanted to get up and run knocking him over in the process.

She looked at Emma. Her mouth could no longer formulate words, but her eyes asked, "Why?"

"Serena, I know you may be upset with me right now, but I felt it was important for you and Nick to talk."

She put some money on the table, got up, reached over and hugged Serena, then said, "Have a safe trip back, and write to me when you are settled." She kissed her on the cheek. "I really miss you, girlfriend, I'll have to vacation home soon so we can hang out together." While Serena stared speechless at Emma leaving, Nick slipped into the seat she vacated.

The silence was awkward. Serena could not look at Nick; so she looked down at her plate and made holes with her fork in the un-eaten French fries, ashamed of the tears that would come pouring out of her if she looked at him. Nick seemed uncomfortable, too.

The waitress reappeared. "Can I take the dishes, please?" She placed the check on the table. Nick looked at it and gave her the money that Emma had left.

"Can I get you anything, sir?"

"Yes, I'll have lemonade with a lot of ice, please."

Finally, Nick spoke. "Serena, I know you are upset, but I was glad Emma called. I really wanted to see you to say I'm sorry." With the fries and the fork gone there was nothing for her to do with her hands, so she turned her head and stared off, refusing to make eye contact with him. Nick continued, his voice shaking. "Things weren't supposed to happen the way they did, it was only supposed to be an arrangement. It's hard to get decent paying jobs without work papers. I was barely able to save with the little I was making, and I thought I could speed up the process for us to be together." He paused, trying to choose his words carefully.

Serena finally had the courage to look up at him as he continued. "Ray and I became friends; we worked on the same night shift at an electronics warehouse in Queens. But I wanted to get back to my passion. I am a good auto mechanic, that's what I wanted to do. So he told me about his cousin Sheila from Puerto Rico. He asked her to help me out and she agreed. After we got married, Sheila started coming around, and hanging out with me and Ray at my place." He paused again… "Then one thing led to another, and she got pregnant." Nick was silent for a while as he nervously twisted the paper napkin. "When she told me she was pregnant, I was devastated." He looked at Serena with pleading eyes. "You have no idea how much I struggled with the guilt. Then, she wanted to move in with me. I couldn't say no, because I didn't want to upset her; I was afraid she would change her mind." He covered his face with his hands briefly. "The plans I had for my future included you and Benny, you have to believe me, but things just didn't turn out the way I wanted them to, and I am so sorry. I stopped writing because I couldn't lie to you anymore."

By then, tears flowed down Serena's face, dripping onto the table. She covered her face as the waitress came back and placed the lemonade in front of Nick. She pulled some tissues from the holder and dabbed her eyes and nose, and finally looked at Nick for a long while. He looked sad, genuinely sorry.

"Please say something, Serena. You could say you hate me, I deserve it."

Staring at a red stain on the white table cloth, and without looking up, she said, "Nick, you have no idea the risk I took to come to be with you." She felt a surge of anger rising inside her as she continued. "My uncle gave me the money from his life savings to make the trip, because they also believed in you." She was angry at herself for being so gullible. Her eyes narrowed as she looked at him. "I felt betrayed when I found out what you did."

Nick looked away. "I have been thinking about you and worrying since the day you showed up at the apartment and met Sheila. It hasn't been easy for me either."

Serena covered her face with her hands and whispered, "I have had such difficulties; it's as if everything is against my being here.

Aunt Julie used to say, "When one door closes, another door opens. In my case I am still staring at the closed door."

"This is a hard place, Serena. The reality is that most people struggle to make it to that Dream."

Serena studied the face she once caressed and the eyes that once had a mischievous twinkle that made her smile. "Are you happy, Nick?"

He thought for a moment and said, "Not really, but I am doing the right thing by Sheila and my daughter." He looked down and continued, "I was happy in Belize, with you and Benny. I've learned that sometimes what we want is not always what is best for us. I got the green card, I am working as an auto mechanic, but it is still difficult. I have to work a second job on the weekends, because one is not enough to take care of my unplanned family. I miss the pace back home. I miss how simple life was, and I miss you and Benny." Serena saw the tears now welling up in his eyes and she felt sad for him. He continued, "I feel responsible for what has happened to you, how my selfishness has affected your life."

Serena's thoughts turned toward Benny, who would no longer be a priority in his father's life, and she felt the tears coming on again. As she gathered her things to leave, she said, "I'm beginning to see the green card as a double-edged sword. People risk their lives, families are separated, relationships are destroyed, and otherwise honest people lie, cheat and suffer humiliation for the sake of it… To be in this land of opportunity comes with a very high price."

Nick picked up a small bag she hadn't noticed before. "I bought some clothes for Benny." He handed the bag to her. Then, he reached into his jacket pocket and took out an envelope. "Here is some money," he said, reaching across the table, and placing the envelope in her hand. "I promise I will support Benny as best I can."

"When will you tell your wife about us?" Serena responded sarcastically.

"I will tell her today; no more lies.

Nick accompanied Serena in a taxi back to Penn Station. They didn't speak much, each quiet in their thoughts. He assisted her with the suitcase to the train platform, and when they said good-bye, he embraced her. She smelled his cologne as her face rested against his shoulder, but it was not the familiar scent of the Nick she knew and loved, and his arms around her did not bring on that total surrender. It was like being embraced by an old friend. He kissed her on the cheek, whispered, "I'm sorry," turned and walked away. She stared after him, but Nick never looked back.

The images rushed past her gaze as the train picked up speed after leaving the station. Serena thought, just as there were many illegal ways to enter into the country, there must be equally as many illegal ways to remain in the country. Nick had chosen an avenue that was probably the easiest and most acceptable, unlike the fool-hearted choice she had made. She wondered what kind of impact it would have on 'the land of opportunity' if all the undocumented immigrants did the right thing and left by their own volition. She had met many individuals who were living and working in the country illegally, some for as long as 10 years. They had become an integral part of the skilled and unskilled workforce. They had established communities, birth children, and were contributing to the economic fabric that made America great. What would be the economic impact if there was an exodus of people willing to do the right thing?

Later when Eric picked Serena up from the train station; he saw that she was in a somber mood and asked, "How did everything go?"

"Fine, I'll be getting the passport in the mail in a few days." She was quiet for a long while then said without looking at Eric. "I saw Nick today." Eric did not press, he could identify with her pain.

Chapter 15

E ric slowly turned his head to look at the clock on his night stand; it was 12:19 a.m. He had climbed into bed at 10 p.m., struggling to turn off the thoughts racing through his mind, the same thoughts that had made him restless and distracted at work all day. Since picking up Serena from the train station and hearing of her plans to leave as soon as she received her new passport in the mail, a sense of gloom had engulfed him. He took a deep breath, rearranged the pillows to support his back, leaned his head against the headboard, and looked around the dark basement he called home.

Twelve months ago, when he had moved into this tiny space, he was angry at God. Despite all his efforts to do things right, everything had gone wrong in his life. He was alone, his wife had rejected him, his son had cerebral palsy, and he was witnessing the mental deterioration of his father, the man he deeply loved and admired. Inside, he felt as dark as the basement. His mother had been his biggest supporter, constantly praying for and with him.

Eric had fought for his marriage, willing to go to counseling or to do whatever Jamie wanted. But she insisted that the marriage had died, that it was not his fault, it was the way things happened sometimes. It all enraged Eric. He understood that she was emotionally and physically drained from taking care of Adam, and that the multiple hospital admissions, surgeries, nursing care and therapies had taken its toll on the marriage. He wished at that time he could have been at home more, away from his demanding job. But they needed his income and medical insurance coverage for Adam. Thankfully, Adam was now four and although he still faced physical challenges, the worse was behind him.

When it became clear that the marriage was over, his mother discouraged him from renting an apartment. "Come home, son, you shouldn't be alone now anyway," she had said to Eric. "Use the basement as an apartment, save your money, and take all the time you need to sort things out." He was grateful for her kind offer, but moving back home was humbling for him. He recalled the first morning there, his father, who no longer recognized him, attacked him in the kitchen with an umbrella. Driving to work that day, his spirit shattered, Eric couldn't stop the flow of tears. He sat in his car for a long time lamenting about everything wrong in his life.

In the days following his move, he realized how difficult it was for his mother to take care of his father, who was as dependent as a baby; however, she never complained. Eric offered to pay for an Aide to come in to help her during the day, but she refused to accept any help. His father used to call her a stubborn Italian.

"He becomes agitated with strangers and very anxious whenever I am not around," she told Eric. Friends from church had been helping her until Eric moved in and volunteered to do the weekly food shopping and errands. The senior pastor stopped by occasionally with sermon tapes since Mrs. Reilly was no longer able to attend church.

As time passed, Eric was beginning to feel better emotionally. Working on a new project to improve the electrical systems on commercial airplanes helped to keep his mind engaged. The divorce had been final for four months, with Eric enjoying every other weekend and a few hours on Wednesday with his son. He never imagined loving another person as much as he loved Adam. His relationship with

Jamie was civil; she had gone back to work part time since Adam was now in school half days.

Eric glanced at the clock again; it was 12:59 a.m. During the past 3 months, he noticed the dark cloud that had been hovering over his life was gone. His mother had said that he was getting the spring back in his steps, and more recently he knew why he was feeling better. She had come into their lives in a very strange way, hiding in his work van, running from the law, injured, and in need of a place to recuperate. They had shown her kindness and in return this stranger had enriched their lives in so many ways. Now, the thought of her not being around, the thought of her leaving, caused him to be anxious and confused.

It was 1:30 a.m. Frustrated that he couldn't fall asleep, Eric climbed out of the bed and dredged up the flight of stairs to the kitchen. His mother always left a dim light on for her occasional midnight trips to the kitchen to get warm milk for his father. When he reached the top of the stairs, halting in front of the doorway, he saw Serena standing near the kitchen sink, with a glass of water in her hand, staring out the window at the darkness. She turned and looked at him, the light reflecting on half of her face. "Having difficulty falling asleep?" She asked almost in a whisper. Eric leaned against the door frame, staring at her dressed in his sister's yoga pants and T-shirt, her thick, wavy black hair flowing around her face. Looking at her, he felt as if a warm wave was slowly flowing through his body, and it suddenly came to him that he was in love with Serena. This woman who had such a gentle spirit … who had helped him to feel alive again … who loved his son … who helped his mother get the respite she needed. He loved her.

Eric walked over to Serena, took the glass from her hand, placed it on the counter and wrapped his arms around her. "I'm missing you already," he whispered. She laid her face against his naked shoulder and returned his embrace. In the quiet of that early morning, they embraced in solitude. When they finally pulled away, they looked into each other's eyes, and they both knew. Serena left the kitchen first, without saying anything. Eric poured himself a glass of milk and returned to his room in the basement. He settled into bed again, this time with a sense of peace, knowing the direction his heart was headed. When his physical longing took his mind in another direction, he whispered, "Whatsoever things are pure, whatsoever things are lovely......think on these things." He smiled to himself, pulled the blanket to his chin and soon drifted off to sleep.

❧ ☙

The remaining days at the Reilly's were bittersweet for Serena. She was excited about going home, reuniting with Benjamin, being in a familiar place where she did not have to worry about her status and personal freedom. Yet, she was leaving the place that could provide a good life for her and her son. She was sad to leave Mr. and Mrs. Reilly, Adam and Eric. In the past few months, she had learned valuable life lessons and discovered spiritual guidance to catapult her maturity as a young woman. When she arrived at the Reilly's, the circumstances of her life were weighing her down. But now she was optimistic and ready to use her energy to rebuild her life.

Eric was occupying her thoughts more and more, especially since they were spending more time together as he helped her with flight arrangements and shopping for gift for her family. His kindness, thoughtfulness, integrity, sense of humor, and those dimples in his cheeks when he smiled, were only a few of the many characteristics she admired in Eric Reilly. She had seen his strength and his vulnerability. She felt attached to him emotionally, and saying goodbye to this special relationship was going to be difficult.

Eric confessed one evening that he looked forward to coming home because of their time spent together talking at the kitchen table. He knew everything about her life in Belize, the history and diverse culture of the country, the ancient Mayan ruins, the rain forests, the coral reefs and white sand beaches. "Sounds like paradise," he would say. She knew everything about his childhood, the teen years when he was enthusiastic about his religious beliefs, and the college years when he began to doubt those beliefs and became a bit rebellious. Spending time with Eric and his son on the weekends gave Serena a taste of what her family would have been like with Nick and Benny, had her dreams become reality.

She was scheduled to leave three days after receiving her passport in the mail, departing from Connecticut, and connecting in Miami for the flight to Belize. On Wednesday night, she went out to dinner with Eric and Adam, and said a tearful goodbye to the little boy she had come to love as her own son. After taking Adam back to his mother, Eric and Serena strolled under the moonlight through Hatters Park, holding hands, basking in this poignant time together.

Eric spoke softly, but with passion, occasionally tightening his grip on her tiny fingers as he told her that she had influenced him to put his energy into rebuilding his life. He had been in a dark place, depressed, lonely and paralyzed by rejection that lingered. Now, he was drawn to her sweet charm, her daring spirit and her unblemished heart. "My mother loves you," he said. "She thinks you were sent to us." They stopped walking and sat on a bench, facing the pond.

They were both quiet for awhile. "It's been a wonderful time for me too," she said finally. "Words cannot express my gratitude to you and your mom." They continued to sit. Serena stared at the reflection of the lights dancing on the surface of the water, remembering another time and place when she was staring at the same thing filled with anxiety. But now there was peace and contentment as she nestled closer to Eric.

🕸 🕸

Mrs. Reilly was up and busy in the kitchen in the early morning hours on the day of Serena's departure. By the time Serena went down to the kitchen, she had made breakfast and packed a snack for her. When it was time to leave, Mrs. Reilly embraced Serena, thanked her, kissed her and prayed out loud for blessings on her life, on her son, and protection on her journey home. As he entered the kitchen, observing Serena standing in the arms of his mother, Eric was suddenly aware of her quiet beauty. Until then, he had paid attention to her heart, her soul, the genuineness of her character. Now, he saw her beautiful, flawless face, hazel eyes, well defined lips, and her thick wavy hair, which she always kept in a ponytail, but today was flowing around her neck and shoulders. She appeared to be taller; he looked down and saw that she was wearing boots with three-inch heels. As his eyes continued up, he admired the curves of her body in the jeans and fitted T-shirt.

On the way to the airport, Serena and Eric glanced at each other and smiled occasionally, but said very little. Eric wrestled with his thoughts, fearful that the feelings of loneliness he dreaded would return. He wished for a severe thunderstorm or some ridiculous reason for the flight to be delayed or cancelled. He wanted the circumstances to be different. There was something wonderful in his grasp and he was being forced to let it go. He pulled the car up to the departure gate of the airline, "Well, here we are," he said, without his usual smile. They got out, he got her luggage out of the car, and neither of them knew what to do next. It was an awkward moment, then Eric held her by the shoulders, looked into her eyes and said, "I love you." He wrapped his arms around her, kissed her on the lips, then abruptly walked away leaving Serena swaying from the passion he had ignited in her. He quickly opened the door of his car and got in. She looked at him through the door, her face revealing her deep sadness. He stared at her intently one more time, then waved goodbye.

Serena had a window seat on the airplane on her flight from Connecticut to Miami. She gazed out the window avoiding glances and pleasantries with the man dressed in a business suit sitting next to her studying pages of graphs and charts on his lap. It was a beautiful day at 30,000 feet above the ground. The sun's reflection on the clouds made them gleam and illuminate. The airplane was flying under the pale blue sky and above the cumulus clouds that looked like large puffs of cotton balls clustered together. The serenity of the scene outside, the humming of the engine, and the gentle movement of the airplane, put Serena in the mood of reflection. She felt the effects of Eric's words, his embrace and the kiss, over and over again and butterflies milled about in her stomach each time she remembered the moment.

She was elated at the revelation that Eric loved her, and that she loved him, but every hour that went by that day took them further away from each other, and the hope of a loving, lasting relationship they both wanted. Then, she remembered Mrs. Reilly's words, "We have the circumstances, He has the Might." She closed her eyes several times that day and entered her fantasy world, a world she hadn't visited much since high school, but now it was different, the tall, dark and handsome man was real not imaginary, and there were two perfect little boys.

Chapter 16

Home at last. Serena looked around the terminal for familiar faces as she made her way to the baggage claim area.
On the flight from Miami to Belize, she wondered about
changes in the country in the two years that she had been away.
Apart from becoming independent from British rule, had the country made any economic progress that would create jobs and opportunities for young people like herself? The luggage from the flight
was in the baggage claim area within 15 minutes; she picked up her
heavy suitcase from the carousel and walked out of the airport terminal to get a taxicab to the bus terminal in Belize City for the ride
to San Ignacio.

As soon as she stepped onto the curb, two taxi drivers approached her. "Taxi for the pretty lady?" One of them asked politely.
The other was more forward, he took her suitcase, and pointing to
his car several yards away, said, "Come, pretty lady, I'll take you
where you wanna go." The other driver politely got out of her way
and she followed the man with her suitcase. As they approached
his taxi, she heard, "Vanilla," then the honking of a car horn. Serena turned around quickly and saw her friend Valerie standing next
to a small white Toyota, waving her hands. "Milk Chocolate," she
shouted back, surprised and happy to see her long-time friend. She

apologized to the taxi driver, took her suitcase from him and headed over to where Valerie was parked.

"Welcome home!" Valerie embraced her warmly.

"How did you know I was....?"

They both lifted the heavy suitcase into the already open trunk of the car. As she navigated the winding roads out of the airport, Valerie explained that Aunt Julia had told her the flight number, date and time of Serena's arrival.

"Since I have my very own car now, I couldn't let my best friend return home on a bus. I took the day off to come and welcome you home."

"Thanks for being so thoughtful," Serena responded.

Valerie grinned. "Purely selfish reasons... I am so happy that you are back, I really missed you. Just wait until you see your son, cute as a button, and he knows it." She paused, and with a mischievous twinkle in her eyes, she said, "So, tell me everything. We have an hour and a half. I'm all ears."

Valerie's facial expressions and comments were comical as always, but as Serena described the events in her life during the past two years, Valerie listened intently, and expressed empathy. As they neared San Ignacio, Valerie exclaimed, "Wow... girl, you could write a book!"

"Comedy? or tragedy?" Serena laughed.

Then, she became quiet and looked out the window at the familiar scenes of her hometown. After a long pause, she continued. "When I ran out of options and realized that I had to come home, my greatest concern was the difficulty of finding work." She reminded Valerie of the hardships she faced before she left. "How will I support myself and Benjamin?" Valerie parked the car on the side of the road near the front of Aunt Julia's home. She looked at Serena as if she already had a plan.

"Well, there is a strong possibility that you could have a job very soon."

"Really?" Serena's eyes widened with surprise."Where?"

Valerie was enjoying her reaction. "Well, I got a promotion at work, and when your Aunt told me that you were coming home, I asked my boss if he would consider you for my old position."

Serena's jaw dropped, she reached over and hugged Valerie. "Thank you."

"Yes ma'am, you have an interview on Monday for the receptionist slash customer service position at the Bank of British Honduras."

It was 6:30 in the evening when Serena walked up the path leading to the house. The sun was disappearing on the horizon, but it was still light enough for her to see everything around her. She stood on the porch of her aunt and uncle's home and looked around the familiar yard; nothing had changed. The gate at the beginning of the walkway to the house was still missing the top hinge; the first two steps on the wooden stairs to the porch were still rotted away at the sides. The rocking chair on the porch where Uncle George smoked his pipe in the evenings had the same worn cushion. Much had happened in her life, but time had stood still at this sea blue painted cement house, with its red front door. She took a deep breath and felt a sense of peace. "Home," she whispered. Standing on the porch, Serena knew that she was now more equipped to handle life's disappointments, and she was ready for whatever came next.

She took another deep breath, opened the front door and was instantly engulfed by the familiar aroma of spices coming from the kitchen.

"Hi, everybody, I'm home!" she shouted, putting down her handbag and suitcase in the middle of the room before heading toward the kitchen. The door that separated the kitchen from the rest of the house swung open and Aunt Julia came out wiping her hands on her apron.

"Serena!" She rushed towards her with outstretched arms, hugged and kissed her on both cheeks. "Look at you," she said, pushing her away and looking at her from head to toe. "You look so much like your mother now."

The door swung open again. It was Uncle George with Benjamin following closely behind him. "Your mamma is home, Benny boy," he declared as he turned and picked up Benjamin. Uncle George hugged her, kissed her, and handed her son to her.

"My baby," she whispered as she kissed his cheeks and spun around the room hugging him.

"You must be tired and hungry, come," said Aunt Julia, holding her hand and leading her into the kitchen. When they had settled down to eat dinner, her aunt and uncle told her funny stories about Benjamin, their faces light up and it seemed that they enjoyed taking care of him. In those initial hours, however, Benjamin was quiet and shy, quite contrary from the precocious little boy everyone described. He sat in her lap during the meal, but when he left the table to play, Serena became solemn and told her aunt and uncle about Nick and some of the circumstances that led to her return home.

On Saturday morning, the busiest shopping day in San Ignacio, Serena took Benny and headed to Burns Avenue to the market place where vendors from other small towns and villages proudly displayed their colorful array of fruits, vegetables and crafts. The air permeated with the smell of spices and ethnic foods being cooked in the small shops and restaurants, lining the crowded streets. Serena did not realize how much she had missed the smells, sights and sounds of this old, tropical town with its colonial style buildings, narrow streets lined with shops, Mayan heritage and the interwoven cultures of Spanish and English. They stopped at a small shop for two of her favorite things: tamales and coconut water. She chatted with old friends and acquaintances, and then returned home with a bag of her favorite fruits: mangos, papayas, bananas and a pineapple.

On Monday morning, she interviewed with Mr. Williams, a soft spoken man who looked down more at the pen he twirled between his fingers than at her as he spoke. The job required a high school diploma, which she had. Mr. Williams remarked that she came highly recommended, and Valerie was such a valued employee that he trusted her judgment. She was relieved that he did not ask her a lot of personal questions. He handed her a copy of the job description, offered her the position and asked if she could start the next day. It was great having her best friend Valerie train her. She learned quickly, which freed Valerie to get on with her new position.

The week after she arrived, Serena wrote letters to Emma and Mrs. Reilly to let them know that all was well with her, and to thank them again for their kindness. Writing a letter to Eric, however, took many days. Apart from thanking him for his unbelievable acts of kindness, she did not know how to put into words her affection for him. She was beginning to feel that Eric Reilly was out of her league. He had a successful career as an electrical engineer, and was a good-looking, Irish-Italian. She had barely graduated from high school and was an out-of-wedlock mother who had displayed poor judgment and naivety with her life. She was sure that the distance between them would soon erode the love he had expressed that day at the airport, as it had with Nick. But she still felt light-headed each time she remembered that kiss and the intense longing in his eyes.

After procrastinating another week, she completed a very generic letter as if writing to a friend, sharing details of how she resumed life in Belize. She stated that she missed him and Adam terribly and hoped that things were going well for them. At nights, with Benny sleeping next to her, Eric occupied her thoughts, and memories of the times she spent with him and Adam replayed in her mind, over and over again.

Surprisingly, in the months that followed, Eric wrote regularly, providing brief synopsis of what was going on with the family. He sent beautiful hallmark cards that expressed his love and longing for her. His letters brought her joy; she started yearning to find his letter waiting for her at home. In one letter, Eric reported that Mr. Reilly had a stroke and his health was deteriorating rapidly. Then, shortly after that letter, she received a call from Eric at the bank with the sad news that Mr. Reilly had passed. She could hear the grief and sadness in his voice. "I wish you were here," he told her.

The days following the news were cheerless for Serena, she was deeply grieved over his passing and wished she could be there with the family. She wrote a letter of condolence to Mrs. Reilly, who she imagined was grief stricken.

❧❧ ❧❧

Soon, life in Belize resumed as if she had never left, except for the longing in her heart for Eric. Although she was with her son, she also missed Adam and wondered how he was progressing with walking. Serena settled into the routine of work, attending church with her aunt on Sundays, helping with household chores, gardening alongside Uncle George, socializing with Valerie and friends. Aunt Julia continued to take care of Benny during the day, because he was still too young to be in school. On Fridays, work ended at 3 p.m., so she was home earlier to spend time exploring the river, rain forests and ancient ruins with Benny and teaching him about his cultural heritage.

On the first bank holiday since Serena started working, she and Valerie planned to drive to the coastal town of Gales Point to spend the day on the beach with a mutual friend. That morning, however, they had to cancel their plans because Valerie's mother became ill. Serena decided to spend the morning going through the box of clothing and personal items that Emma had mailed to her. Most of the clothing was not appropriate for the warm Belize weather, so she separated them into smaller boxes and put them under her bed.

In the afternoon, Benny came to her with his ball and bat. He was wearing his favorite blue cap, Serena followed him outside. It was warm with a slight breeze, and since the sun was facing the back of the house, the front yard was shaded and cooler. Aunt Julia sat on the front porch embroidering on a large piece of white fabric to be made into a tablecloth; the women's ministry group at her church was making linens to send to missionaries in Africa.

Benny held his bat, ready to hit the ball. He missed hitting it the first time and several times after, his frustration growing with every swing. Serena moved closer to him and his bat finally made contact with the ball, which hit the gate and bounced into the street. As she ran to get it, she noticed a taxi cab coming slowly up the road toward the house. She paused for a moment and stared. Benny called enthusiastically, "Come on, Mommy, let's play." She was about to turn her attention back to Benny and the game when she heard, "Serena!" The sound of that familiar voice made her heart do a back flip in her chest. Then, she saw his smiling face out the window of the taxi; it was Eric.

He was out of the car in an instant. She dropped the ball and rushed to him. They embraced, then he lifted her off her feet and swirled her around. When he put her down, he held her face in his hands, looked into her eyes and said, "I have really missed you." He kissed her on the forehead, then embraced her again. For a moment, time stood still. The taxi driver turned off the engine. "What, what a surprise," she stuttered, catching her breath. Then she heard, "Ce," just above a whisper. Serena's heart leaped with joy as she looked into the taxi and saw Adam, smiling and struggling to get out. Reaching in, she lifted him out, and held onto him. She began to cry, overwhelmed by happiness at seeing them both again. "I can't believe you're here. Sometimes I wondered if I would ever see you again," she said, looking at Eric. When she finally put Adam down, he looked up at her smiling, "I missed you, too."

By then, Benny had moved closer and had a confused look on his face. Serena brought the two boys together for introductions, while Eric paid the driver and got Adam's crutches from the back seat of the cab. He looked at Serena with the boys. His mother had said that she would be a wonderful wife, a woman who would love and respect her husband and create a loving, peaceful home for children. He had never felt so sure of anything in his life. Eric walked over and gave Adam his forearm crutches so that he could balance and walk by himself. Serena was amazed to see him walking so well. When she stood up, Eric took her hands. They stared at each other for a moment. Then, he said earnestly, "I love you Serena, and I want us to make the journey through life together. So I came all this way to ask you to be my wife. Will you marry me?"

Serena was speechless. She looked at the boys walking together, Benny talking to Adam and leading him toward the house, where her aunt and uncle standing on the porch were staring at the scene unfolding in front of them. She looked back at Eric, and remembering his unwavering kindness from the day he discovered her in the back of his van, she smiled, "I love you too, Eric Reilly." Then she shouted, "Yes! Yes! Yes!" She threw her arms around his neck, and he embraced her. Serena closed her eyes, savoring the moment, and thought... *"Sometimes, when one door closes, another door opens and happiness comes through."*

About the Author

Jacintha, also known as 'Pearl' to her childhood friends, was born in St. Georges, Grenada in the West Indies. Grenada, the "Island of Spice" is a small island of 133 square miles located in the eastern Caribbean and is north east of Venezuela.

Ms. Griffith left her homeland in February 1979 on a vacation to visit family in Toronto and Winnipeg, Canada and Brooklyn, New York. While in Winnipeg, she saw the television broadcast that a political revolution had erupted in Grenada. That revolution would later be one of President Reagan's foreign policies, as he sent in US troops for an invasion in October of 1983. Ms. Griffith continued with her planned vacation stop to Brooklyn, New York, and while there she made the decision not to return to her homeland where political instability was prevalent. She and her husband, who 5 months later had joined her in the U.S., faced the difficulties and uncertainties of obtaining legal residency. While navigating the many legal avenues to remain in the United States, she heard various interesting stories of how people dealt with the barriers to citizenship. Years later, while sitting at her desk on the 67th floor of 1 World Trade Center where she worked as a staff financial analyst, she looked across the Hudson River at Brooklyn with its culturally diverse immigrant population, and this story began percolating in her mind.

Ms. Griffith worked for 11 years for the Port Authority of NY and NJ in the World Trade Center, leaving her position as a staff financial analyst with the Treasury department in July 1996 to attend

New York University's Masters of Occupational Therapy program. She has been working as an Occupational Therapists since January 1999 and has lived and worked in New Jersey, New York, Florida and Texas. She has developed a passion for social and educational issues since working with young children with physical disabilities, as well as for the issue of immigration, after working with children of migrant families in Florida. Ms. Griffith received a humanitarian award in January 2009 from the Ocala Florida Elks/Florida Elks Association for her service to children in Marion County.

Ms. Griffith, has 2 grown daughters. She currently lives in New Jersey. This is her first novel.

Ms. Griffith states that if there is a single sentence that describes her life, it would be this one from a song written by Bill and Gloria Gaither:

"I walk into the unknown, trusting, all the while."

Special Thanks

To my daughters: Tammy and Katrina for encouraging me to publish. And special thanks to Katrina for patiently helping with all my technical questions.

Roger Campbell: Who edited the manuscript, and provided valuable feedback. "Be more descriptive" is one of his comments I will always remember for future writing.

Sue Collier and her team at Self-Publishing Resources, for guiding me through the complicated and detailed process of self-publishing a novel.

Singer and song writer, Andrae Crouch, for permission to use the words of his song, "Through it all" in the story.